"I am in love with you."

"But—you can't be!"

"Why? You are quite lovable, you know."

"But—" Mattie knew she must put an end to this declaration. He had taken her hand in his strong, masculine one, and the strangest things were happening to her palm. A tingling had invaded it, as if her hand had been frozen and now was thawing. . . .

"I am older than you," she managed to choke out, even though her speech was hampered by a shortness of breath. She must be firmer. "You are nothing but a boy."

A glint lit his eyes. "It has been many years since a woman's called me that. . . ."

# THE
# BUMBLEBROTH

## Patricia Wynn

FAWCETT CREST • NEW YORK

A Fawcett Crest Book
Published by Ballantine Books
Copyright © 1995 by Patricia Wynn Ricks

Library of Congress Catalog Card Number: 95-90030

ISBN 0-449-22364-7

Manufactured in the United States of America

First Edition: July 1995

10  9  8  7  6  5  4  3  2  1

# Chapter One

$\mathcal{L}$ady Westbury put down her needlework to stare over her pince-nez at her son. It was not often that she either took the time to examine him or had it, for Lord Westbury had the habit of residing in London, while she passed the year at his country seat. Just now, he was perusing the newspaper he favored instead of obliging her with a game of cards; but as usual he had managed to turn down her invitation to play in such a manner as to get what he wanted while making his refusal seem the greatest compliment to her.

Ordinarily his skillful manner when dealing with her would have annoyed Lady Westbury immensely, but tonight she reflected that it was fortunate he had such address. Without exaggerating, she could tell herself that he was a credit to the Nortons in many ways. His face, for a gentleman of thirty who had lived for no other reason than to please himself, was remarkably free from signs of dissipation. Some, his mother conceded, might even call it handsome. His dark good looks had come from her family, of course, for the Nortons were never known for their beauty.

If there was a certain severity to the cut of his face, and something formidable about his tall stature, both of which gave him an air of authority, she could only approve them. Both had come from her. The only qualities he appeared to have got from his late father were his unfailing courtesy and his tendency to levity. The latter, of course, she deplored, for he often used it in thwarting her wishes.

Still, she mused, it was possible that an impressionable young lady might find something in it to admire.

It was time, Lady Westbury had decided, to take a hand in managing her son's affairs. It was all very well for a young gentleman to have several years upon the town, but after a reasonable period it was his duty to stop enjoying himself and to think of his family instead. In this, Lady Westbury was perfectly willing to help him, since now it appeared that in doing so she could kill two birds with one stone.

"It is good you are come home just now, William," she said to him in portentous accents.

Lord Westbury peered over his newspaper with a wary expression.

"My dearest Mama," he said, a thin veil of warning slipping over his eyes. "Such warmth overcomes me. If I were a suspicious person, I daresay I should be alarmed by such a spontaneous burst of affection."

"Nonsense!"

Rising to the bait, Lady Westbury picked up her stitching again and applied herself to it with force. "You say that to tease me, William. You know that I have always been most affectionate towards you—not but what you have often been unappreciative of the little attentions I've troubled to pay you. If I sometimes appear cold, it is merely a reflection of the dignity I feel to be due a peer of the realm. You will undoubtedly thank me for my forbearance in these matters one day."

"Undoubtedly," said her son.

Lady Westbury went on as if she had not heard him. "But how I am to show any affection for one who visits seldom and, when he does, only stays for one night, I cannot imagine!"

Perceiving that William had gone back to his newspaper, she called to him sharply and reminded him that she was still speaking.

Lord Westbury put down his paper with a sigh. "My most profound apologies, madam. You were saying . . ."

"I was saying that it is good you are here at this moment. You are undoubtedly unaware that the Dowager Duchess of Upavon has taken up residence at Westbury Manor."

"My deepest felicities," William said, turning back to his paper.

"You miss the point, foolish boy!" His fond parent lost all patience with him. "I insist you put down that paper and listen to me until I have indicated that I am finished speaking."

"I will listen with pleasure," Lord Westbury assured her, setting aside the favored paper, "but I fail to see that the duchess and her residence have anything to do with me."

"Naught to do with you?" Lady Westbury arched her brows. "When I have told you repeatedly how your grandfather, the third viscount, lost that very piece of property to the sixth duke in a card game?"

"Ah, yes." William kept his eyebrows admirably still. "How foolish of me to forget that."

"Just so," Lady Westbury said, mollified. "I am certain I have told you of the circumstance countless times. By all reports, your grandfather was not himself when he sat down to play, and the duke should never have taken advantage of him."

"Three sheets to the wind, wasn't he?" William inquired politely.

Her ladyship wrinkled her nose. "I really could not say."

"Rather the worse for a shove in the mouth as I heard it," William mused. Then, seeing his mother bristle, he added, "But perhaps it is unwise for us to speak of one of the Nortons in such a fashion. One should say rather that Grandpapa was a bit *on the qui vive* or simply 'ticklish.' "

Lady Westbury glared at him. "That is neither here nor there, William, and I will thank you to keep the language of the boxing parlor out of my drawing room."

"Certainly, Mama."

He appeared to be going back to his newspaper, so she said quickly, "I have not finished. The point is that the property was taken from your grandfather under the most dubious of circumstances, and I have often felt it was a grave injustice to your family."

"Even though half the properties in England have changed hands under similar circumstances?"

"Nonsense!" Lady Westbury crossed her hands

primly in her lap. "You would have it, I suppose, that we are a nation of drunkards and card thieves! Not, of course, that I would ever refer to your grandfather in such a way, William, for I never had the pleasure of meeting him."

Lord Westbury inclined his head. "It would not be far from accurate, all the same."

Lady Westbury gasped. "I know what is due to your father's family, William, even if you do not!" She added petulantly, "But all of this is beside the point. You are trying to distract me."

William gave her his full attention, but his indifferent expression was far from encouraging. "Then by all means, Mama, let us come to the point so that we may retire to bed. I have a busy schedule tomorrow."

In the interest of progress, Lady Westbury swallowed a retort. "What I have been trying to say is that the duchess has taken up residence on the property that ought to have been yours. The old duke bequeathed it to her daughter. That is why you've come at such an opportune time."

William's eyes narrowed, and his manner became more distant. "What a peculiar set of statements. But somehow I feel certain you mean to enlighten me as to their relevance."

"Of course I mean to do so. So you will oblige me, please, by showing some interest. If matters were just—which they never are—I should expect you simply to tell the duchess how grotesquely unfair it was to sever the property from your estate. But that would never serve." Lady Westbury dismissed this idea with a reluctant sigh. "No—the reason it is good you are home is because this will be the perfect time for you to fix your interest with Lady Pamela."

William's tone grew cooler. "Lady Pamela? Would she, by any chance, be the daughter in question?"

"Yes, of course."

"And may I ask how old the young lady is? I seem to remember that the Duchess of Upavon was considerably younger than her husband."

"*That* would be putting it mildly," Lady Westbury snorted, distracted by the opportunity for gossip. "As I recall, the gel was barely sixteen herself when the old fool married her. Quite a scandal there was about it at the time—and no wonder! It is shocking to think of a man of his consequence being trapped by no more than a slip of a gel! And for his money, no doubt!"

"Perhaps he wasn't trapped at all," William said mildly. "The way I heard it, the old duke was never fond of women. Perhaps he wanted an heir."

Lady Westbury scoffed. "Well! If he did, he made a great mistake, didn't he, by marrying such a young gel? She only bore him the one daughter, so what was the use in it?"

"He may have cared for her."

This provoked a titter from William's mother. "What notions you do have, William! As if the old duke would marry for affection! I'm certain if it was affection he wanted, he could have got it anywhere. There are more important considerations for marriage, I can assure you."

This turn in the conversation brought Lady Westbury's mind back to her original purpose, and with a shake of her head, she chastised herself for letting the subject wander.

"But that is neither here nor there, William. The duchess's marriage need not concern us at the moment. It is her daughter I am speaking of!"

"As I recall," her son said helpfully, "you were about to tell me the age of this child with whom I am asked to fix my interest."

"She is fifteen or thereabouts; it does not signify. She is the owner of Westbury Manor, and her dowry will undoubtedly be attractive. The essential consideration is that she lives retired, for her mother is quite a recluse, which should give you a clear chance to establish yourself in Lady Pamela's affections without fear of competition."

Lord Westbury's lips curled upward. "Your confidence in my charms is, as always, most gratifying, Mama."

"Don't be ridiculous, William! I am certain you are quite capable of convincing the young lady of the desirability of the match. You have no need to fish for compliments."

Given the plans she had formed on William's behalf, Lady Westbury was glad she had nothing to worry about with respect to his success with women. She preferred to hear nothing about his more distasteful exploits, but she was gratified to know that many a matchmaking mama considered her son, the viscount, an answer to prayer. Nor were their daughters loath to stand up with him at a ball or to be escorted by him into supper. But, so far, William had not shown a decided partiality for any one of his partners.

Lady Westbury had always thought it a shame

that her handsome looks should be wasted on William. Gerald, her second son, had taken after the Nortons, which was unfortunate since, without the likelihood of inheriting a title, he had more need of a pleasing countenance to make an advantageous match. William, of course, having inherited the viscountcy, needed no such enhancement.

Pursuing the subject, she added, "It will just be so much easier to fix your interest with Lady Pamela now before she is launched upon the world. Who knows what fancy might take her if she suddenly is exposed to society? I have never been one to believe in love matches, but I do hear the most alarming tales about girls these days."

Sensing the displeasure emanating from her son's side of the room, Lady Westbury stiffly offered, "If you doubt your own attractions, William, I must tell you that I have heard rumors of more than one broken heart that can be laid at your door. You are a tall, athletic man. Your taste in clothes is impeccable. And I am not so far removed from society that I do not know the value of a well turned-out leg."

Her son gaped at her in astonishment. His voice, when he spoke, sounded feeble. "Mama, you positively unman me! Such encomiums from you! I had no idea you thought me such a paragon!"

She gave him a spiteful look. "You are toying with me, William, and I will not have it! Just remember that I am counting on you to do your utmost to attach Lady Pamela!"

Lord Westbury carefully folded his paper and rose from his chair. He bowed low to his mother.

"I am extremely loath to disoblige you, as you must know, Mama, but I am afraid my schedule will not permit a courtship at the moment. I am due in town on the twelfth, and even you, with your highly flattering belief in my powers of attraction, cannot expect me to woo the young lady in just one day."

He seemed to think the discussion at an end, but Lady Westbury had prepared herself for just such a case of rebelliousness. She threw him a triumphant glance.

"To be certain, you cannot court her in one day. But you shall come with me to call upon them in the morning, for I have promised us both to the duchess!"

Lord Westbury stared down at his mother. In these days, it was seldom that she managed to get the better of him, for he spent as little time at home as possible. It was a gentleman's prerogative to spend as many or as few days on his estates as he wished. William's infrequent visits, always unannounced, were enough to make certain that his property was being properly managed, but he had long ago decided that he would prefer to conduct his personal affairs without his mother's interference.

For the first time that evening, he smiled unpleasantly and appraised his mother in a way that made her shift uncomfortably.

"Very clever, Mama. You know me well enough to suppose that I'd not purposely put you to the blush. Very well, I shall go. But I should let you know that I find the notion of a man of thirty pursuing a girl of fifteen somewhat less than palatable. And she will have to be something far out of the ordinary to attract my interest. I have no mind to shackle myself to a child. Tomorrow evening I shall be leaving again for London."

He bowed again and wished her a good night.

As he strolled to the door of the drawing room, Lady Westbury dismissed his last words and set about thinking how to overcome her son's absurd objections.

# Chapter Two

*H*aving agreed to accompany his mother, William was prepared to do so pleasantly, knowing it was fully in his power to defeat her current project by simply returning to town once the call had been made. Therefore, in the morning he obliged her by driving her himself in his chaise and pair, his groom perched up behind.

They arrived at Westbury Manor in a matter of minutes, and William prepared himself for an annoying but commonplace event. Many times he had been presented to young ladies recently released from the schoolroom. None of them had inspired anything more lively in him than an avuncular feeling, and he had acquired a comfortable manner of dealing with them and putting them at their ease. This manner was so unloverlike that the girls' mothers usually perceived at once that the case was hopeless and pursued the connection no further.

William had been cornered by hopeful mothers often enough that he half expected the duchess to be a party to Lady Westbury's matchmaking scheme. But this notion was quickly laid to rest by the reception he and his mother received at the dowager's door.

Her Grace's footman seemed quite at a loss as to what to do with morning callers. After taking their names and leaving them on the doorstep long enough for Lady Westbury's dignity to be offended, he passed them along to an elderly butler, who received them with discouraging politeness.

"I am afraid Her Grace is not receiving callers this morning," he informed them.

William lifted an amused eyebrow at his mother, who, under his scrutiny, turned a distinct shade of red.

"I thought you said we were promised to Her Grace this morning, Mama? Perhaps you mistook the day."

Lady Westbury stiffened. "I never make mistakes." Then, addressing the butler, she said, "You will take our cards to the duchess, if you please, and conduct us to a room where we may await her comfortably. I am certain she has merely forgotten our appointment."

"As you will, your ladyship." The butler relented with a disapproving glare. "I shall see if I can find Her Grace."

With that cryptic remark he showed them into the morning room and vanished, presumably in search of his mistress.

Lady Westbury took a chair and gazed about the room, purposely avoiding her son's eye.

"I have never known you to be misinformed about your appointments, Mama." William was enjoying his mother's discomfiture immensely.

"Nonsense! He will find the duchess directly and that will be the end of it." Lady Westbury bobbed her head sharply in a gesture of dismissal. "I daresay she simply forgot. It was a very casual arrangement between us, so I see no reason to harp upon it. I count on you not to annoy the dowager by bringing her error to her attention."

"It will be as you wish certainly, Mama, but it is strange, is it not, that I was so thoroughly convinced Her Grace would be expecting us?"

Lady Westbury did not take the bait on this occasion, so William sat down in an armchair and read something to hand while they waited for the duchess. From time to time Lady Westbury made some proprietary remark in a loud whisper to him about how well appointed the rooms were, or how she would alter the furnishings if this were her parlor. To all of these, William offered no reply other than to smile at her in a disagreeably knowing way.

They waited for what seemed like a very long time. The clock ticked loudly on the mantel, pointing out the uselessness of their venture. By the time they heard the sound of approaching footsteps, Lady Westbury had noticeably begun to fidget, though she would never give up her mission once embarked upon it.

In the end, it was not the butler who appeared, but a very different sort of person altogether. The door to the garden opened, and a lady entered the morning room, a small-boned creature with that sort of English fairness that is always accompanied by rosy cheeks. The brisk breeze that blew that morning had raised the color beneath her pale skin to give the appearance of roses set in alabaster.

She strolled through the door, humming a little tune, and checked suddenly upon the threshold. Her blue eyes, set in a heart-shaped face, widened with dismay. A hand flew to her lips.

"Oh, dear!" she said on an indrawn breath.

It was easy to see why she was discomposed, for she was certainly not prepared to receive visitors. She carried a quantity of cut flowers in both hands, so many that her sudden stop caused half a dozen of them to fall upon the floor. She tried snatching at them but, in doing so, lost twice that number.

The flowers were not the only evidence that she had been gardening, for a rather significant quantity of dirt clung to the hem of her gown and to the pair of tattered gloves she wore. A smudge of earth appeared on the end of her nose.

Clearly she had groomed herself with the expectation of being dirtied, for her fine, blond hair had been drawn up upon her head as if to get it out of the way rather than to achieve any particular style. Half of it had rebelled against this haphazard confinement and fell in silky strands about her face.

Her dress showed a similar lack of concern. Her gown was old and outmoded, a flimsy confection of muslin with a low bodice and narrow skirt, dating, William guessed, from her girlhood, when *les merveilleuses* had been the fashion leaders in Paris. A bosom of pleasing maturity appeared above her décolletage, set above an attractively small waist.

Considering her untidiness, a man of less perception might have been excused for thinking he had been intruded upon by the scullery maid; but William noted a certain grace to her movements and an unmistakable air of quality in her carriage. A quick estimate of her age and her casual air convinced him of her identity.

Seeing that surprise had paralyzed her for the moment, William stepped forward and stooped to pick up her flowers. He held them out to her with a bow.

"Your flowers . . . Your Grace?"

She blushed and tried to take the flowers from him, losing another dozen in the process.

"Oh, do forgive me!" she said. "I am not always so shatterbrained. But you see, I was not expecting visitors!"

William cleared his throat, but refrained from glancing at his mother, who instantly exclaimed, "How awkward! Well! Perhaps I ought to have written a note to remind you, duchess, but it does not really signify, you know, for we are here now."

Her Grace of Upavon seemed perplexed by this rambling statement, but she overlooked it and, assuming her role as hostess, begged them both to be seated again.

"I would be delighted," William said, "but something tells me I ought to present myself first. I am Westbury."

The duchess colored again and smiled up at him shyly. "Of course. How foolish of me not to think of it. For of course, we never have been presented, have we?" Her fair skin responded readily to even the slightest hint of a social blunder.

"Now that we have met, I hope you will forgive me for appearing in this fashion. I always garden in the morning, so I am not normally home to visitors. But perhaps Barlow did not inform you?"

"If you mean your manservant," William said, coughing discreetly for his mother's sake, "I'm afraid he tried, but we were not so easily discouraged."

The duchess looked at him questioningly; but before an awkward silence could result from William's attempt to bait his mother, Lady Westbury took command of the conversation.

"Westbury can only be here for a very few days, duchess, so we thought we should take this chance to call in the hope of seeing dear Lady Pamela." Her voice dwelt fondly on Lady Pamela's name, so much so that the duchess was clearly taken aback.

"To see Pamela?" she repeated. She looked back and forth from William, who had achieved a distant expression, to Lady Westbury, who was smiling at her most intently.

"Yes, of course." Lady Westbury tittered in what was meant to be an encouraging way. "I have spoken so often of Lady Pamela in my letters to William that he has declared himself quite wild to see her! You must not hide her from us forever." She wagged a finger at the duchess.

Her Grace of Upavon gazed openmouthed at Lady Westbury for the better part of ten seconds. It was clear to William that this playful mood of his mother's had struck the duchess as unnaturally as it had him. Privately he thought that Lady Westbury's charade had gone on long enough, and he was prepared to call an end to their unexpected visit if only he could do so gracefully.

But then the duchess surprised him.

She stopped staring at Lady Westbury and turned toward William with a suddenly hostile eye.

William met her look with a bland countenance, concealing the fact that he understood what was behind her shrewd expression. She had tumbled to his mother's interest in a match between himself and Lady Pamela and was trying to measure his complicity. He thought he recognized the look. The duchess could only be interested in appraising him as a suitable husband for her daughter.

To most mothers of young ladies, his visit—given the size of his estate and his standing as a peer—would have been immediately welcomed. But it soon became clear that the dowager duchess was not so easily won. After some moments of silence—during which the duchess's look changed from mere guardedness to an expression of active resentment—William was at pains to hide his amusement. A smile tugged at the corners of his lips, which did not escape her notice.

She flushed and turned to speak to Lady Westbury firmly. "I'm afraid you have been put to a great deal of inconvenience for nothing. At this hour, Pamela will be occupied with her lessons, and I would not wish you to wait while she prepares herself to meet visitors."

This excuse would be quite inadequate to discourage Lady Westbury, as William could have told her. Surprised—and slightly piqued—that the duchess had found him wanting, he abandoned his intention of leaving and settled down with pleasure to watch the coming confrontation.

The duchess, for all her firmness, was a delicate seedling to his mother's hearty vine. If any of his wagering cronies had been present, William would immediately have put one hundred pounds on the likelihood that Lady Westbury would prevail.

"Oh, we would be only too happy to wait for her," Lady Westbury cooed. An underlying steel gave the lie to her tone. "You should call your man and tell him to ask Lady Pamela to come down. He left us to wander about in search of you and never returned. It will do him good to be set a task for keeping us waiting so shamefully."

William was quite accustomed to his mother's rudeness, but the duchess heard her with astonishment. The criticism on the politeness of her staff could hardly be ignored. It required her to call the butler at the very least. This she did, and then waited in rigidly smiling silence for the servant to answer.

The snub had no effect on Lady Westbury, but William, feeling that it was merited, set about making pleasant conversation, to the end that he managed to coax at least one smile from the duchess before the servant appeared.

By the time the elderly Barlow had entered the room, Her Grace of Upavon had sufficiently recovered under this gentle treatment to do further battle in her daughter's behalf.

"His lordship and Lady Westbury would like to see Lady Pamela, Barlow, but I have informed them that my daughter is probably immersed in her studies or, I daresay, even resting. Would you happen to know?"

She exchanged a meaningful look with her servant, who, after betraying only a glimmer of surprise, said after a slight hesitation, "Your Grace is undoubtedly correct."

The duchess turned back to Lady Westbury, folded her hands in her lap, and smiled, blissfully unaware of the dirt on her nose. "You see," she said, "Pamela must be occupied."

William hid a smile. Her triumph—grossly premature, if she only knew—could only goad his mother to greater rudeness.

"Nonsense!" Lady Westbury declared, more in keeping with her normal manner. "We shall wait until he has carried your message upstairs."

The duchess bit her lip, obviously unaccustomed to such an accomplished adversary. William felt a strong urge to explain to her that this lack of tact on the part of Lady Westbury constituted his entire reason for living in London the year round.

Nonplussed, the duchess turned back to her servant. "But I daresay the governess will be most annoyed if Pamela's lessons are disturbed. Don't you agree, Barlow?"

"I quite agree, Your Grace."

Lady Westbury huffed. She gave Barlow the look she used to depress all pretension in servants. "You must not let yourself be bullied by the child's governess, duchess! I would not, for one moment, tolerate such a thing in my household!"

Finally at *point non plus*, the Duchess of Upavon turned to William as if for assistance. She still clutched the flowers in her hands; they had long since wilted.

William debated for a split second whether to respond to her silent plea and call an end to the encounter, but by this time he had begun to enjoy himself far too much. He knew that he would do no harm to Lady Pamela, no matter what the duchess thought. Her reluctance to present the girl had made him start to wonder just what sort of *nonpareil* she was hiding. His intentions could not be altered; no girl of fifteen could interest him enough to hold his affection. But if the girl had even half her mother's beauty, he would count it worth the trip merely to have seen her.

Besides, it piqued him to know precisely what the duchess had found in him to make him so ineligible. He was not accustomed to being thought lacking. Curiosity and his rather cynical nature, at this point, got the better of him.

"I must confess—" William clasped his hands behind his head, crossed his legs, and settled himself more deeply into his chair "—the longer the wait, the more eager I become to see her."

There was a pause while the duchess's eyes grew round with dismay, but William's last words finally seemed to decide the issue. With a startled breath, Her Grace of Upavon immediately instructed her servant to inform Lady Pamela that visitors wished to see her. Then, as an afterthought, she told him to make certain that Nanny Phillips accompanied her charge.

"My daughter is scarcely out of the nursery," she informed them with her chin in the air.

This offended posture gave William a better look at her enchanting profile, but he could not resist provoking another flash from her blue eyes.

"The nursery? But I understood Lady Pamela to be some fifteen years of age. Surely it is unusual for a girl of fifteen to be in the care of a nurse?"

The duchess colored as if he had caught her telling the biggest bouncer of her life.

"Nanny Phillips has been in my service since well before Pamela was born," she explained rather vaguely. "I regard her more as a companion for Pamela than as a nurse, but my daughter is—*still*—quite young enough to be in her charge."

There seemed nothing to say to this, so William leaned back in his chair and awaited the entrance of the mysterious Lady Pamela.

Lady Westbury filled the interval with boasts about the Norton family, something she took pleasure in doing on even less pertinent occasions. From time to time she threw a compliment to her son, which he did his best to ignore. It was clear that his apparent about-face had placated her, so that she was willing to overlook the teasing barbs it had pleased him to send her way.

Before too many minutes, the door opened to admit Lady Pamela, accompanied by Nanny Phillips. They were followed by three or more fine hunting dogs, who came so closely in Pamela's wake as to seem almost a permanent escort. Remembering them as she advanced into her mother's morning room, the girl uttered a sharp sequence of commands. The dogs immediately sat at attention, their adoring gazes fixed firmly on their mistress's face. So well mannered were they, they never once took the slightest notice of the guests.

Pamela's quick entry only served to confirm William in his suspicions, coming as it did a mere five minutes after her summons. Evidently Lady Pamela had been neither resting nor studying too deeply. She had the air of someone who had been out and about for hours.

William rose and made his bow to the girl and the elderly nurse at her side.

After so much preamble, however, Lady Pamela's appearance came as something of a disappointment. She was certainly no beauty to be guarded from moonstruck suitors. In spite of a pleasant openness of countenance, she did not favor her pretty mother in the least, unless the paleness of her hair could be ascribed to the duchess. But unlike her mother's silken strands, Lady Pamela's were curly to the point of being frizzy. They surrounded a round face possessing none of the duchess's delicate features. Her skin, though fair, was of the sort that tended to redden under embarrassment rather than turn a rosy pink. Her figure, too, being on the stout side, lacked the elegance that would find favor with most gentlemen. She was dressed in a simple but fashionable gown that did nothing to hide a rather masculine stride.

William did not let any hint of his disappointment cross his features, but immediately put himself to the task of setting the young lady at ease. He could see she was not accustomed to strangers. She curtsied most awkwardly.

From his own mother, this lack of polish would have drawn an instant wince and a subsequent rebuke when the company had departed, if not sooner. He half suspected he had tumbled upon the reason for the duchess's attempts to put him off; surely she would have wished to prepare her daughter better for such a meeting.

But glancing at the duchess's face to see how she was taking her daughter's clumsiness, William found no criticism of Pamela's performance. Instead, he saw in the mother's look only a rather touching protectiveness, as if she were blind to her daughter's deficiencies.

Since William's mother had no right to govern Lady Pamela yet, she only winced mildly at the child's awkwardness. Then she covered her grimace with an embarrassing plethora of admiring phrases, encompassing the child's hair, her face, and her gown. The more she effused, however, the more annoyed the duchess appeared and the redder Lady Pamela's face became, so William offered the poor girl his arm and conducted her to the window seat to spare them both his mother's compliments.

Nanny Phillips followed them and stood at her charge's elbow. She was, if anything, even older than Barlow—a shrunken, wizened, almost fairy-tale creature, who looked as if she might have been spawned by an acorn. William warmed to her instantly, but noticed that she was striving to hide a yawn as if she had just been wakened from a morning nap. Her cap was put on neatly, though, and she fulfilled her, perhaps, unaccustomed duty in good form.

Quite pleased with her son now, Lady Westbury did her best to hold the duchess captive by engaging her with impertinent questions about Westbury Manor.

After seating himself beside the young lady, William made several attempts to draw her out with the ballroom chatter he had perfected on other girls of a similar age. She responded to him awkwardly and with an obvious lack of interest. Her complete deficiency in social skills at first amused him, and then rapidly grew tedious. He began to wonder why the duchess had been so determined not to expose her daughter to his notice, for surely there could be no danger of his falling in love with the chit. His mind was increasingly taken up with this question, to the point that he was at pains to find something to say to Lady Pamela, until a chance remark of his about his horse brought a gleam to the girl's eyes.

"Are those your horses in the stables now?" she asked excitedly.

"The pair of grays? Yes. They brought us in my chaise. Did you see them?"

"Oh, yes." She sighed on a note of bliss. "Mama's head groom called them to my attention when I came in from my ride this morning. He knew I would wish to see them."

*So much for the governess story,* William thought, wondering again at the duchess's reluctance. "And did they meet with your approval?"

"Such prime bits of blood? How could they not! They are bang up to the nines!" At a reproving sound from Nurse, who had come awake at such language, Lady Pamela covered her mouth. "Oh, sorry. I'm not supposed to use expressions I pick up from Tim."

"Is Tim your groom?"

"Yes."

"Then I quite see that he would not be the best person to emulate."

He was rewarded with a giggle. Happy to find a successful topic, he continued, "So you admire horses, do you? And you ride. Do you drive a team?"

Lady Pamela gave a scoffing laugh and waved him away with a most indelicate gesture. "Of course not, silly," she said. Evidently, now that she knew William to be a good judge of horse-flesh, she was willing to accept him as a friend. "Whomever should I get to teach me? My mother rides, but Papa never allowed her to drive a team, and Coachman is far too old and deaf." She sounded rather wistful.

"Well, perhaps I could teach you," William said, thinking in passing that the house seemed remarkably full of old retainers. "If I decide to stay in the country for a time, I would be happy to call and take you for a drive."

He wondered what on earth had induced him to make such an offer. He had begun to like Lady Pamela, but certainly not to the extent that he would change his plans for her. She was an honest, engaging child, free from all the affectations he so earnestly detested in other debutantes. As engagingly unaffected as her mother, in fact, but without a particle of her beauty.

"Oh, would you?" Lady Pamela responded gruffly, reddening with pleasure at the thought. "That would be just the thing!"

Nanny Phillips made another tut-tutting sound. William promised Pamela to make his best effort, and then told her stories about his younger brother that he thought would appeal to her. Gerald was the most bruising rider in the family. In spite of his thin frame, he had a "neck-or-nothing" courage that got him over every fence without a spill. He seemed to speak a horse's language, so that he was able to extract the best behavior out of the most poorly mannered beast. William reflected that it was too bad Gerald was not yet down from Oxford.

As she listened to his stories about Gerald's prowess, Lady Pamela's eyes shone with excitement. But after a while William was at pains to hide the fact that the task of entertaining her had grown tiresome. From time to time he glanced surreptitiously at the duchess and found her straining to listen to her daughter's conversation. The spot of dirt still bedecked her nose, and she had long since given up on her flowers. The sight of her daughter's eager receptiveness to William's interest seemed to trouble her, and before long she found a means of bringing their tête-à-tête to an end.

Interrupting Lady Westbury, she rose and said firmly, "I am afraid you will have to pardon me, but I think Pamela has had enough society for one day. She will more than likely be tired from all the excitement."

Pamela looked surprised and started to protest, but the duchess turned to Nanny Phillips and asked, "Isn't that right, Nanny?"

Nanny Phillips hesitated only a second over the unfamiliar question. "That's right, Miss

Mattie—er, Your Grace," she said. "I was just thinking it would be time for Pammy's nap."

Pamela's face betrayed signs of a sustained shock that revealed she was not used to being considered such a baby.

William ignored them and, turning toward the duchess with a lift to his brow, repeated, "Miss Mattie?"

Her eyelids fluttered. "Yes, my name is Mathilda," she admitted ruefully. "Nanny has been with me since I was His Grace's ward, you see, and occasionally her tongue slips. She is inclined to forget, from time to time, that I am no longer her charge, but she still takes very good care of us."

She regarded Nanny Phillips fondly and with only a mild exasperation for having betrayed her. Even the duchess, at this point, could no longer pretend that Lady Pamela was still confined to the nursery.

She gave her daughter permission to retire. Lady Pamela gave a sharp command to her dogs, and tails waving, they jumped to follow her from the room. Nanny Phillips curtsied to the company and bustled Lady Pamela out. Before she could do so, however, William promised Pamela to return soon for their driving lesson.

"But—I thought Lady Westbury said you would be leaving!" the duchess cried, in accents clearly indicating she felt herself to have been deceived.

William gave her the slightest of bows. "My plans are uncertain. Would you object to Lady Pamela's riding out with me in my chaise?"

She looked anxious. "I couldn't possibly permit such a thing unless I accompanied you."

"Of course," William said, bowing to hide a smile.

Within minutes of this exchange, Lady Westbury and William took their departure. Lady Westbury carefully guarded her tongue, but only until William's carriage had passed through the gates. The instant it did, she began enumerating all Lady Pamela's virtues, the amenities of the property she had inherited, the income she believed to derive from the estate, and the advantages to the Norton family if there should be a match with the daughter of a duke.

Then, unable to restrain herself, she passed on to the duchess's eccentricity and the outrageousness of her costume.

"I was never so shocked as when she walked in from the garden!" she exclaimed. "That gown! I declare I have not seen anything like it since those shocking days before His poor Majesty fell ill. Why, it scarcely covered her! I would rather be struck dead than to appear in such a garment!"

Then, with a quick glance at William, she added hastily, "But you mustn't let the duchess's conduct discourage you, William. After you are married, you can find her another house somewhere. You needn't think she will be a burden. Just don't permit it."

Lady Westbury carried on in this vein for some time, before noticing her son's silence. He had neither commented on any of her observations nor told her his plans for the morrow.

Anxious to discover just how successful her

scheming had been, she prompted, "Well, William. You have said nothing at all. Have you no answer to give me?" She turned in her seat the better to observe his expression.

William came out of his abstraction. "My apologies, Mama. I did not realize you were speaking. What was it you wished to know?"

"Not realize that I was speaking! How can you say such a thing, William, when I have been informing you of my feelings this past quarter hour! I have been wondering what you thought of her!"

"Of the lady?" he said in a distant tone. His face revealed no earthly clue as to his sentiments.

"Of course, I am asking about the lady, if it pleases you to speak in such terms! Tell me instantly what you thought of her!"

William commented absently, "I confess that my interest is piqued. I thought her charming—and rather clever."

"Well!" Lady Westbury settled herself back into her seat with an air of satisfaction. She had known William would come to his senses and see the advantages of the match, but she had not cherished any hopes that he would be smitten with the girl. After all, Lady Pamela was hardly what one would call beautiful. If William found her interesting, however, she would say nothing to disabuse him of the idea, for she knew gentlemen were peculiar in their tastes. And to call Lady Pamela clever . . .

"William—" she scooted forward again "—I hope you did not misunderstand anything Lady

Pamela said to you. I can assure you that she is not a bluestocking. Far from it!"

Her son gave a mischievous grin. The sight of it was vaguely disquieting.

"Oh, no," he said. "I don't fear that. Lady Pamela does not concern me at all."

# Chapter Three

As soon as Lord Westbury and his mama had driven out the front gate, Her Grace of Upavon, Mattie, gathered up the skirts of her flimsy gown and ran up the stairs to find Nanny Phillips. As she did so, she noticed the wilted flowers in her hand and, uttering an expression of dismay, flung them over the balustrade. Then, remembering that her footman was getting too old to stoop, she ran back down to collect them and disposed of them herself.

She found Nanny alone, dozing quietly in a chair in her private sitting room. Mattie crept up to her on tiptoes.

"Oh, Nanny darling," Mattie whispered. "I'm so sorry, but do you have to nap just now? Oh, please wake up, dearest!"

Nanny came awake with a jerk, clearly thinking that one of her former charges had screamed during the night with teething pains. Mattie gave a guilty hiss and applied herself to the task of calming her old nurse. After a few moments of this tender treatment, Nanny came fully to her senses, saw where she was, and invited Mattie to take a chair. But the duchess, suddenly aware of the dirt on her gown and gloves, knelt at Nanny Phillips's feet instead.

"What did that horrible man say to Pamela, Nanny? You must tell me everything. I've been dying to know!"

"There, there," said Nanny, pushing her spectacles back onto the bridge of her nose before patting the duchess's hand. "He didn't say anything you need get in a pet over. He just talked about his horses and the like."

Mattie gasped. "But nothing could be worse! Then what about Pammy? Did she seem to—to take to his lordship?" She searched for reassurance in Nanny's pale, old eyes.

Nanny shook her head, bewilderment clouding her features. "Well . . ." She pondered for a moment. "Pammy liked all that talk about driving his team, I could see that."

Mattie bit her underlip.

"She went on a bit rough at first—" Nanny nodded indulgently "—but you know what she is—not much one for gab, unless it's about something she do care about." Nanny's face brightened. "But I'll say one thing for his lordship—he tumbled onto our Pammy's likings right away and told her all about his nice pair of grays. Just the right sort of chatter for our Pammy!"

Mattie uttered a little sound of distress and rose to her feet. She stood there indecisively for a moment, nibbling one fingertip of her glove.

"What is it, pet? What's got you all adither?"

Mattie started. "Oh, it's nothing, dearest. I oughtn't to have bothered you." She bent and planted a kiss on Nanny's shriveled cheek. Then she drew Nanny's shawl back around her shoulders and, after apologizing for disturbing her rest, begged her to go back to sleep.

A few moments later, she peeked into the schoolroom, uncertain whether she would find Pamela engaged with her governess. But apparently Lady Pamela had not taken her mother's excuses at all seriously and had escaped once again to the stables. No one was in the schoolroom but Lady Pamela's governess, Miss Fotheringill.

She turned until Mattie could see the cool gray eyes beneath her clear brow and trim lace cap.

"Come in, Your Grace," she said, giving Mattie a serene smile of welcome. Miss Fotheringill was the only retainer, with the exception of Barlow, who always remembered to address Mattie as she should, not from any lack of familiarity or affection, but out of a strict desire to accord Mathilda the proper degree of respect due a duchess. Miss Fotheringill had instructed Mattie, too; and if, at times, she found it difficult to refrain from demonstrating too much affection for her employer, she was always careful not to reveal such an improper inclination in public.

Miss Fotheringill stretched out an elegant hand and bade Mattie sit in the chair by the fireplace. Even though spring was nearly at end, she kept a fire always burning in the grate. Her room was a warm haven, which Mattie never failed to seek when something troubled her.

"Oh, Gilly!" Mattie burst out, not bothering to conceal from her governess what she had barely hidden from her nurse. "I've had the most disturbing call!"

"Oh, dear. Not Mrs. Puckeridge again."

The rector's wife was a notorious gossip, as they had discovered within a few days of taking up residence at Westbury Manor. She called with regularity, and it was in part because of her annoying visits that Mattie had declared her policy of not being at home to anyone.

"Not Mrs. Puckeridge, no. It was Lady Westbury and her son, Lord Westbury."

"And how did they distress you? I know Lady Westbury can be rather overbearing, but I had not thought you so easily overset."

"But she was quite rude! She criticized Barlow and me and you— But that is neither here nor there, Gilly," Mattie said, putting those issues aside. "What matters is that they most particularly asked to see Pamela."

"But why should they not?"

"They practically demanded to see her! Well . . ." Mattie considered. "Perhaps it was Lady Westbury who did the demanding. But her son did nothing to discourage her. He let her bully me until I could do nothing else but call Pammy down, and then he told me how eager he was to see her! If you could have seen his smug expression!"

"Smug? About what?"

"That's just it! I could tell they were up to something. If you could have seen Lord Westbury's bland look! I was certain he was laughing at me. And his mother—why, she was behaving in the most extraordinary fashion! But I could see at once that she had designs on Pamela."

"Designs?"

Mattie hunched her shoulders miserably. "I believe she wants my Pammy for her son."

"But what does this all matter?" Gilly said, consolingly. "You would never give your consent to an early marriage, and I cannot believe that Pamela has any thoughts of one."

"That's precisely what I would have said." Mattie's heart trembled for her daughter. "But that was before I saw him."

"Saw who?"

"Lord Westbury!" Mattie stood abruptly and started pacing back and forth in front of the chimneypiece.

Miss Fotheringill observed her agitation with surprise and no small degree of concern. "Why should seeing him make any difference?" she asked, bewildered by Mattie's reaction.

Mattie slowed to a stop and raised her hands helplessly. "Because he is just what every girl dreams of," she said, a wistful note stealing into her voice. "Tall and handsome—and with such considerable address that he could persuade any girl to fall in love with him."

She paused, then gave her head a little shake and resumed pacing. "It astonishes me that anyone with his obvious attractions should even consider courting a child. As if enough girls would not throw their caps at him!"

Miss Fotheringill folded her hands in her lap and watched as Mattie strode up and down the room. Mattie's distress clearly still perplexed her, but before she could offer any comforting words, Mattie caught sight of herself in the mirror above Pamela's desk and came to a halt.

"Eeeek!" In the glass she had seen the smudge of dirt on her nose. She licked her finger and rubbed the spot vigorously. "All that time I thought I was being my most dignified, and instead, I looked as foolish as the undergardener!"

"Do you mean to say you received Lady Westbury and her son dressed as you are?" Gilly's shock could be heard even through her modulated tones.

Mattie looked down at her dress anxiously. "Like this? Well . . . yes, but—of course, I wasn't expecting anyone. You know Barlow refuses all morning visitors because I prefer to do my gardening in the early hours." She held out her skirt and glanced back at the mirror. "But is it so dreadful, do you think? It seems so wasteful to be digging in a new gown. Would Lady Westbury—"

Gilly interrupted her with a delighted laugh. "Yes, my dear. It is positively dreadful! I've cautioned you before that you must take care not to dress as if you've been to a ragfair—even when you are gardening. You must think of your position."

"Oh, dear." As she peered in the looking glass, Mattie's voice matched her wilted flowers. "What must Lord Westbury think of me?"

Gilly stared at her curiously. "I don't see that it matters what he thinks of you."

Mattie felt herself reddening. "No, of course it doesn't matter," she said, remembering how Lord Westbury had stared when she had first entered the room. "But he was so perfectly groomed, you see. Really quite elegant! One could see he was a member of the ton. Whereas I—"

She broke off that line of thought and continued forcefully, "But you are quite right. That's entirely beside the point. The point is that I won't have him sweeping Pammy off her feet before she has a chance to go out into the world. Especially when he doesn't love her!"

There was a pause. "And why shouldn't he love her?" Miss Fotheringill asked quietly.

Mattie glanced up. "It's not that, Gilly. You know it isn't. There is no earthly reason why he should not adore her. He could not find a dearer, sweeter, more forthright child than our Pammy." A lump of sadness weighted her chest. "It's just that she is still a child, and I want Pammy to have some fun before she marries, to have a chance to meet several gentlemen and to choose from among them. I want her to go to balls and routs and musicales—"

She saw that Gilly was staring at her and broke off. A faint pink color rose to her cheeks.

"I think I know what you mean," Gilly said, giving her a distressed look. Then she said hesitantly, "Mattie, dear—Your Grace—I have often reproached myself for not speaking more forcefully before your marriage. I was younger then, and afraid to put myself forward, but I should have spoken to His Grace and insisted on your having a season in London before—"

Mattie spoke quickly. "Oh, no! You mustn't make anything of what I've said. I was truly fond of His Grace. If I had even thought of refusing his kind offer, I'm certain he would not have insisted on marrying me!" She faltered, then went on with a gentle smile, "And we suited one another—truly. I daresay another husband would have put a stop to all my wild habits. It would not have suited me at all to be forced to behave. And I could not very well carry on the way I like in London, could I? The one time I was there, it was most painfully obvious to me that I should not fit."

But Gilly was frowning. She was not so certain, and the uneasy tilt to Mattie's shoulders did nothing to convince her. "You were never wild," she said, not comprehending. "And I flatter myself that you were as well, if not better, prepared for London than most ingenues. If you had made your curtsy before your marriage, you might have enjoyed—"

Mattie averted her gaze and cut across Miss Fotheringill's speech. "Oh, perhaps," she rushed on, "but that is precisely why I should like Pamela to have some fun with other girls her own age. She might make some friends in London, go to the theater and balls, museums and the opera—"

Gilly stopped her, shaking her head with an air of doubt. "It is possible that Lady Pamela will enjoy the amusements of the ton even less than you did. She shows very little interest in such things."

"Do you think not? Oh—you must be worrying about her horses. Well, she may ride in London surely and—" Mattie paused. Then she hugged herself at the elbows and said with a little shrug, "I want Pamela to have the chance, that's all. I want her to meet several young men and decide for herself whom to marry."

"And so she shall." Gilly rose and put an arm about her. "I should not be so quick to imagine

that Lady Pamela will fall prey to Lord Westbury's charms. He must be nearly thirty, at
least—more than ten years her senior. I daresay
that will seem quite old to her."

"But such marriages are made all the time!"

"That is true. But to a girl like Pamela, who
has given no thought to marriage yet, he will appear to be of an age with you."

A startled look came over Mattie's face. Her
eyelids fluttered, and she said rather breathlessly, "Perhaps it will seem so to Pamela, but I
must be far older than he is!"

Gilly laughed. "Of course, you are. Perhaps as
many as eight years. But while that may seem a
vast number, for all practical purposes, you and
Lord Westbury must be considered as forming
part of the same generation."

Mattie said nothing, but still seemed unhappy,
so Gilly said, "Well, no matter. If Lady Westbury
saw you in that gown, she was probably so offended that she will never countenance another
meeting, much less an alliance between her son
and your daughter. I should think you will have
nothing more to worry about."

Mattie looked up as if she had not quite heard
her. Then Gilly's words reached her and she
chuckled.

"And you must not let Lord Westbury upset
you, Mattie," Gilly added more seriously. "Even
if he calls again, you will know perfectly well
how to discourage him. And surely he would not
bring his mama with him the next time! Without Lady Westbury here to push him—and I
agree that she is the most shocking bully—you

will have no trouble sending his lordship about his business."

Mattie heaved a great sigh. "Of course. Thank you, Gilly. You always know just what to say." She mused for a moment. "And even though he does have her rather formidable air, it did not seem to me that Lord Westbury had quite the arrogance of his mother. He was most polite—distressingly so, when I think how easy it would be for him to captivate a young girl. And so relaxed. As if nothing ever unsettles him." She paused and then said doubtfully, "But perhaps he will be willing to take the hint."

"There. That's more the spirit." Gilly released her and turned back to the books she had been perusing.

Mattie stood awhile longer and brought one finger up to her lips. She was still too disturbed to return to her work. An image of Lord Westbury as he had stooped to hand her the flowers entered her mind.

"Well . . . I certainly hope he doesn't come back," she said to the air.

She fell silent for a moment, thinking of the way he had leaned back in his chair. Such a masculine gesture! To Mattie, who had spent her life surrounded by women and elderly men, it had been fascinating.

"Is there anything else, dear?" Miss Fotheringill asked. She was watching Mattie, a frown of concern on her smooth face.

Mattie started and flushed. "Oh, no," she said. "I was just thinking . . ." Her mind wandered again. "I imagine he's capable of turning any girl's head, what with those handsome features. And his manners . . . so engaging . . ."

She sighed and, after casting a look at Gilly, hugged her tightly.

As she moved toward the door, Miss Fotheringill called, "Oh, Your Grace. I suggest that you have Turner make you up some simple gowns to wear for gardening." She looked reprovingly at Mattie, but a twinkle lit her eyes.

Mattie glanced over her shoulder and smiled at her former governess. "I shall try not to disgrace you again, dear Miss Fotheringill."

By the end of the week, when no more had been seen of either Lord Westbury or his mama, Mattie had got over the worry the two had caused her. She decided, however, that she should follow Gilly's advice about her gardening clothes in the event that any of her other neighbors decided to force themselves upon her at such an unwelcome hour. The thought of Pamela's presentation, which must take place sometime in the coming three years, had begun to weigh heavily upon her mind. Her own inexperience in such matters could only complicate the event. The last thing Pamela needed was to have gossip about her mother's want of conduct preceding her to London.

While waiting for her elderly dresser to make up the gowns Gilly had suggested, Mattie could not neglect her garden entirely. Her new rosebushes must be set out before too late in the growing season.

In the secluded life Mathilda had led, alleviated only by His Grace's army of servants and the occasional visit from one of his relatives, Mattie had devoted herself to the cultivation of flowers. This garden, which over the years of her periodic visits had spread and blossomed, had been the reason for her particular fondness for Westbury Manor.

It beckoned her daily, and if the evidence of her labor left its traces on her clothes, it did not really matter. No one was likely to see her, in any case, except the servants she had known since her girlhood. Even His Grace had not minded the occasional smudge of dirt on her face or the touch of sun upon her cheeks. He had seldom commented on her appearance at all except to pat her on the shoulder from time to time and tell her she "looked in fine fettle."

At the moment, Mattie reflected, she must look far from distinguished. She had been digging for the better part of an hour and now was mixing the soil in each hole with her gloved hands in order to bring it to the exact texture she wanted. The picture she made at home was greatly at odds with the one she must present in London as a proper mother and as a duchess.

Though she had recovered from Lord Westbury's visit, she had not been able to shed the lowering thought that she would be perfectly incapable of launching Pamela into society with correct decorum. Her lack of experience oppressed her. She knew herself to be entirely ignorant about the style of gowns Pamela should wear, and she would hardly be assisted by Turner's rather outdated notions. She must give Pammy a ball, but how would she ever choose the most welcome refreshments to serve to their guests? How would she manage to hire musicians and caterers and a whole set of London servants?

She was thinking of all the many details she would have to learn while down on her hands and knees, turning the earth in a deep hole, when a man's shadow fell across the ground in front of her.

She started and drew back on her heels. Lord Westbury stood regarding her from his considerable height.

"Good morning, duchess. I'm sorry if I frightened you." The breeze played with the hair at his temples, lightening the severity of his lean looks. A smile turned the corners of his lips, and Mattie noticed he had a deep indentation in each cheek.

He was dressed for riding. A pair of boots encased his legs from the knees down, and he was carrying an elegant beaver hat.

"Oh, no!" Mattie said a bit breathlessly, starting to rise. "That is, you did startle me a bit. You see, I—"

"You're not accustomed to morning visitors."

He offered his hand to assist her to her feet. She gave hers to him, thinking she had been right when she imagined she had seen a spark of humor in him, so lacking in his mother.

"Yes," he went on, "I recall what you said about your schedule. And in case I had forgotten, your manservant has proven himself quite capable of reminding me. I called only to ask when I might take Lady Pamela for a drive. I

43

thought I might find you both outside at this hour."

His boldness, when she had made it only too plain that she did not receive callers in the mornings, annoyed her, especially when she realized she was covered in dirt again from head to toe. She was wearing another old gown, this one a bit too confining, for it was one she had worn before Pamela was born. She tugged at its bodice self-consciously and hoped that Lord Westbury would not notice its age.

"When you did not return," she said unguardedly, "I thought that perhaps you had gone back to London."

"I did go back." An amused look pulled at the corners of his eyes. "I had an engagement I could not put off. But, as you see, I have returned. Were you—that is, was Lady Pamela expecting me sooner? I hope she was not disappointed."

"Not at all," Mattie said coolly. "Where is your horse?" She looked around and saw no sign of one.

"I left him in the stables with your groom and strolled about the grounds alone. I hope you don't object?"

Mattie refused to absolve him entirely but did not know how to convey the proper degree of displeasure. Obviously his lordship had inherited some of his mother's arrogance. She knew she should give him a setdown, but concern about the way she was dressed would rob it of force. She wiped her nose with a clean spot on her glove just in case there should be another smudge.

"I was gardening," she said.

"So I see." Laughter tinged his voice. His eyes had taken in her dress and gardening accoutrements with one quick glance. Looking at her with a slight lift of the brow, he asked, "And Lady Pamela?" He seemed quite unperturbed by Mattie's cool manner towards him.

"My daughter is engaged, *quite* engaged for the morning," Mattie said. Then she added in a tone that would brook no argument, "For the *entire* morning."

"Ah, I see." Lord Westbury's disappointment was only too patent. "Well, then, perhaps you could suggest another morning for our drive?"

Mattie produced a frown of concentration, as if she were giving the matter serious thought. "Well . . . she is rather occupied lately." She waved toward the upper floors of the house, directing her vague gesture towards the schoolroom. "Lessons—drawing masters and so forth. I would not care to ask you to cool your heels until a more suitable time can present itself." She shook her head and gave him a politely discouraging smile.

"It would be no bother. I assume she rides each day?"

Mattie nodded grudgingly.

"She would not be unwilling, perhaps, to exchange a gallop for a driving lesson?"

Mattie started to deny this, but Lord Westbury cut in swiftly, "I could see that she was quite eager to learn, so shall we say next Tuesday? I expect my brother, Gerald, will be down and could join us if you have no objection."

Mattie found herself in a quandary. She was

not certain whether, if she objected, she would be objecting quite rudely to his brother's joining them, or to the outing itself as she intended. Then she realized that whether his brother came or not, she could not invent any reasonable excuse for refusing Lord Westbury's offer. She could only accept with a cool nod.

She expected Lord Westbury to depart then, but when she made signs that she was ready to return to her work, he surprised her by saying, "Could I be of any assistance?"

His question caught her off guard. She stared at him, trying to understand his latest machination. She was still irked with herself for giving in so meekly to his proposed drive.

"I'm quite the enthusiast for plants myself," he said before she could refuse him.

"You are?" Mattie regarded him suspiciously. "That comes as a great surprise to me, my lord, for I understood that you made your residence in London the year round."

Amusement seemed to hover at the corners of his eyes, but his expression quickly changed to one of innocence.

"That is quite true," he said. "And, of course, I cannot indulge my . . . er, passion in London as much as I would in the country. I can only do so here."

"You will not want to soil your riding clothes."

"Ah, yes—" he considered "—then perhaps I shall just watch you. I'm bound to learn something. And you mustn't let me disturb you. If you happen to need a hand, I'll be ready to help."

Mattie hesitated. The warming sun reminded

her of all she ought to accomplish that day. She was almost certain she understood his motives. He intended to stand about in the event that Pamela might come within view. Then he would try to bully her into letting Pammy ride with him. Mattie fervently hoped her daughter would not appear outdoors within the next hour, as she was quite likely to do, once she had hurried through her lessons in order to enjoy a morning's outing.

"Very well," Mattie finally said. She could not think of a way to discourage his lordship from staying—not without resorting to his mother's degree of rudeness. She determined, however, not to let his presence annoy her. At least she had succeeded in keeping him away from Pamela for the moment.

She resumed her digging, and Lord Westbury lay down on the smooth turf nearby, his booted legs stretched out comfortably before him. One of his solid heels tipped over the rosebush she had been about to plant. He appeared not to notice as he picked a blade of grass to nibble on while glancing about the garden. From time to time his gaze returned to her, and when it did Mattie felt her movements falter.

It was not that he watched her with any particular obtrusiveness, but for some reason she found it difficult not to fidget beneath his gaze. The bodice of her ancient dress stretched tightly across her bosom, and its skirt had the irritating tendency to inch up at the hips. She pulled at it from time to time, between giving vicious stabs to the earth.

After a few minutes of this, Lord Westbury

cleared his throat. "Your garden is lovely, Your Grace. I assume you had much to do with its design."

His compliment pleased her. The work she did was for her own enjoyment, but she seldom had the pleasure of sharing the results with anyone else. Aside from the gardeners, no one in her household took much interest in her flowers. Her attempts to engage Pamela in this pursuit had failed miserably, losing inevitably to her passion for horses.

Mattie smiled her thanks, then reminded herself that he might be trying to turn her up sweet to further his own plans. She resisted the impulse to talk about her efforts.

"Yes, I've planned and cultivated everything you see," she said. "But you must tell me about your work, Lord Westbury. What is it that you grow in London?"

A disconcerted look momentarily crossed his features. "In London?" he said. As he hesitated, Mattie grew suspicious. She began to wonder if he had not boasted in order to be permitted to stay.

"Yes," she said, poking at the ground with a growing sense of pleasure. "I presume you have a hothouse. You could not possibly raise anything seriously without a good one. And you cultivate . . . ?"

She directed him a waiting look, enjoying the way he tried to overcome his surprise. He sat up and, clearing his throat again, leaned his elbows on his knees.

"Well," he said, his lean face now hiding any sign of hesitation, "of course, there are the fruits and vegetables served at my table." His eyes shifted uneasily as if he searched his memory for inspiration. "And there are roses, of course."

"Ah," Mattie said encouragingly. "Roses. I am quite fond of roses myself. And what varieties do you grow?"

Lord Westbury looked at her warily. "Red ones," he said after a moment. "And pink ones, too."

Mattie tilted her head to one side. "Red and pink," she said. "How fascinating!"

A reluctant grin spread over Lord Westbury's face. She could see he knew that she was baiting him. But Mattie had begun to enjoy herself, and she was not ready to stop.

Doing her best not to smile, and looking away from him so as not to be tempted, she went on, "And do you grow orchids? I have often wished for the time to devote myself to orchids, but the garden takes so much of my time that I have not been able to learn about them. But perhaps you have?"

"No, duchess, I have not," he said firmly. "As you so wisely point out, the cultivation of orchids takes far more time than one has. I am, however, well acquainted with the varieties of oats and rye and wheat needed to cultivate my acres. I have little time for the more—shall we say— frivolous plants."

"Except roses," Mattie reminded him.

He nodded, a smile curving his lips.

"Well, my lord." Mattie stood and brushed the loosest bits of dirt from her dress. "I have been so grateful for your assistance, but as you can see, I am nearly finished for the day. If you will just hand me that rosebush there beside you, I shall plant it and we can bid each other good day."

Lord Westbury had risen to his feet as she stood and now took a look about him. The rosebush lay to one side where he had kicked it. Its roots were gathered in a bag of soil. Its three-branch trunk was pruned and stripped of leaves.

Mattie watched while he took first one and then a second look at the ground about him, unsuccessfully trying to follow the direction of her gaze. Mattie hid a smile and peered at his face, unwilling to make things easier for him.

Lord Westbury turned back again and raised one eyebrow with an inquiring look.

"The rosebush, my lord?"

"Please, duchess," he said helpfully, "call me William."

The diversion threw her for a moment. She felt herself coloring, but thought it must be the amusement she had been trying so hard to stifle.

"William, then," she said, covering her lips with one finger to restrain them. "Would you be so kind as to hand me that rosebush?"

He followed her glance more ably this time, and his eyes fell upon the neglected bush. He stooped and reached for it.

"Ouch!" he said, and licked his finger.

Mattie pressed her lips tightly together while he picked it up, using more care than on his first attempt. He raised its leafless trunk to the level of his eyes, holding it in a pinch between thumb and forefinger.

"Yes," he said, examining it critically. "I can see that it is indeed a rosebush. But are you quite certain you want it?"

Mattie opened her eyes widely. "Why, yes, William, I think I do. Why do you ask?"

"Because it would appear to be quite dead."

Mattie's smile would not be held any longer. She tilted her head and laughed accusingly at him.

"It is dormant," she said, reaching to take it. "Before they are planted, roses must be pruned of all their foliage. But I am quite astonished that an expert like yourself, Lord Westbury—one who has cultivated both *red* and *pink* roses, if I have not forgotten the precise varieties—that a gentleman of your vast experience should not know that!"

"Ah, yes," William said, smiling to acknowledge how shamefully she had caught him out. "Most likely I should. You will have to pardon me, duchess, for my deplorable memory."

"Not at all." Mattie placed the bush in the hole she had dug. "Your deplorable memory, sir, has afforded me a great deal of entertainment."

William stooped again and picked up the beaver hat he had tossed to one side. He brushed it casually with the cuff of his jacket, placed it at an angle on his head, and then tipped it to her.

"If I have been of any use to you at all, duchess, then I must be eternally grateful." He bade her good day, and Mattie watched him move without hurry across the lawn.

She shook her head and laughed delightedly to

herself. If Lord Westbury had been under the impression that he could deceive her as to his motives, she trusted he knew better now.

## Chapter Four

The next Tuesday morning, William was reading the paper over beefsteak and eggs when a loud thump at the bottom of the stairs heralded the approach of his brother, Gerald. Ready to hurl himself into the day, Gerald had obviously decided to skip the last eight steps of his descent.

A fair, boyish face, perched atop a gangly body, appeared in the doorway and lit up upon seeing William.

"Hullo, Will. Didn't expect to find you here."

"You had better not let Mama see you taking the steps in that manner, or you will receive a brisk lecture on proper gentlemanly behavior."

Gerald started guiltily. "Is she up, then?" He cast a worried glance over his shoulder.

"What a disrespectful thing to ask. Of course, she is not yet risen. Mama is of the opinion that any female who breaks her fast before the hour of ten—noon in Town—must necessarily be vulgar."

Gerald chuckled, but as he strolled to the sideboard, he said with a shade of diffidence, "Oh, Will, Mama is not so bad as that."

"No?" William's brows rose in surprise. "You must be privy to a facet of her character that has been denied me. But," he said, changing the subject quickly, "Mama's character can wait. I am glad you are down, Gerry, as I have a proposal to make to you which involves my team of grays."

Gerald turned to the table, his plate heaped high with fish and strips of bacon. "Your team? You've brought them with you?"

William nodded, an understanding gleam in his eye. "I thought you might be interested. I need your help."

"If it has anything to do with that team, you've got it," Gerald said, straddling a chair. "Where are we going?"

"Not very far. I have promised to give Lady Pamela driving lessons this afternoon."

Gerald gaped and nearly choked on a piece of bacon. "You're going to let a female drive that team? You must be dicked in the nob."

"Flattery, my young cub, will get you nowhere. Do you wish to drive my team or not?"

"Of course I want to drive them. Will I before or after Lady Pamela—whoever she is—ruins them? I'd rather not be blamed for the harm she'll do their mouths."

William allowed a rare grin to cross his lips. "Since you seem to have been spared this knowledge, I will inform you that Lady Pamela is our neighbor. She resides with her mother, the Duchess of Upavon, at Westbury Manor. And you need not fear for my grays if I do not. I think Lady Pamela will surprise you. She seems a quite capable sort of girl. And you will be driving with us during our lesson."

"Me? Play groom to a female? You must be bosky!"

"Gerald, may I remind you that you have just defended our mother to me. I am sure you can discover a buried snip of gallantry inside that thick skull of yours."

Gerald looked anything but comforted. "But why? Why would you want to submit your prime tits, which must have cost you the better part of fifteen hundred guineas, to a lady?"

"She is not a lady yet. She is little more than a girl."

Gerald's brows rose, and a suspicious look came into his eyes. "Not your usual fare, is she?"

"Not at all, but she is that rare sort of girl who shows a complete mastery over her animals. I promised to teach her, and since I have pledged myself, I would like to have your company."

"Can't handle the team yourself?"

William replied with terrible firmness, "I must warn you, Gerald, that such disrespectful language could easily be misconstrued as an insult, which would do nothing to further your own expectations. I might be driven so far as to consider marriage as an option with which to cut you out of the succession."

Gerald whooped. "What gammon!"

"Indeed. I trust you will tell that to our mama."

Not having seen each other for many weeks, the two brothers embarked on a lively discussion, which included the result of the last race meeting they had both attended. The talk became quite heated, Gerald being of the opinion that the horse he had backed, and on which he had lost thirty pounds, had been grossly misridden by its jockey, while William demurred, having backed the winner.

But by the time they pulled up at Westbury Manor and Gerald had been given the opportunity to drive William's grays, he was in high spirits once again.

This time, on knocking, William was greeted as if expected, although he could not fail to detect the disapproval in Barlow's carriage. Recognizing that it would behoove him to make an ally of Mattie's steward rather than an enemy, he set about placating him by being on his best behavior.

He agreed meekly when Barlow announced that Her Grace would be down shortly and asked whether the gentlemen would not rather wait outside "to keep their horses from setting on the fret." William even managed not to grin at this rather clumsy attempt of Barlow's to mimic coaching slang.

Before the ladies joined them, Mattie's head groom, Stocker, limped stiffly out from the stables, ostensibly for the purpose of checking out the harness, although William suspected Stocker could not forgo the opportunity to see such rum goers. William had made the groom's acquaintance on his last call, and had not been surprised to find that he, too, was an octogenarian.

"You'll be needin' a firm hand with these bits, my lord," he said, shaking his head dourly.

"You needn't fear for your mistress, Stocker. Even if I prove to be ham-handed, my brother, Gerald, will bring us about."

Gerald snorted, as well he might, for William was a noted whip. He had set a record time from London to Reading, which still had not been broken. However, Stocker gave no sign of having heard of William's well-earned reputation. He seemed to think that the entire party would be carried home on litters.

The arrival of the ladies put an end to their idling. William presented his brother, and Gerald managed a creditable bow. Lady Pamela, though shy, seemed eager to meet a man about whose daring exploits she had heard so much.

William handed her into the front seat of the phaeton he had brought down for the purpose from London, while Gerald helped Mattie onto the rear bench.

"Now, you hold on, Miss Mattie," Stocker called anxiously from the horses' heads. "If the carriage goes to rolling, you just duck down below that box."

Amused by her groom's familiar address, William glanced over his shoulder in time to see Mattie flush. Had they all known her since her infancy, then?

He did not let himself be distracted by her appearance, although this was the first time he had seen her without a smudge on her face. She was garbed in a blue riding habit that, though dated, seemed hardly to have been worn, and this piece of evidence helped to explain Stocker's unwarranted concern.

The blue became her, bringing out the blue of her eyes and the rose of her cheeks. So much so, in fact, that William found himself curious to discover how Mattie might look in a ball gown of the same hue.

Pamela was eager to begin, so he raised the reins and coaxed the grays down the carriage-way. Gerald had taken the edge off their friski-ness, but still they took a moment to settle in to their paces. Unused to the countryside, they had the tendency to shy at the scurry of every squir-rel or the flutter of every pheasant.

"Are you ready to take the ribbons, Lady Pamela?" William asked, when he thought they were ready for her.

She nodded, so he pulled the carriage to a halt. Gerald hopped down and ran to their heads while William explained the proper way to thread the reins through her fingers.

Watching from the back seat, Mattie strove not to appear too anxious, although the prospect of this outing had loosed butterflies in her stomach. She knew that the way to her daughter's heart would likely be through horses, and she had put herself on guard for Pammy's sake.

Nothing would be simpler for Lord Westbury, Mattie feared, than to exercise his considerable charm while teaching Pammy how to drive. Mattie stood ready to call a halt to the outing at the first hint of flirtatious behavior.

As William patiently placed each of Pamela's fingers where it needed to be, Mattie could not truly fault his manner. There was nothing loverlike in his approach. He spoke to Pammy kindly, much the way His Grace had when teach-ing Mattie how to play whist when she had been of a similar age.

Despite this similarity—or perhaps because of

it, Mattie could not be certain—she felt her worry increasing. A subtle difference underlay the two episodes, but a difference Lord Westbury could not help. He could not be blamed for being so handsome, for having a voice both gentle and low, or for possessing hands that were at once both strong and elegant.

Mattie focused on his hands as he shifted them farther down the reins to support Pamela's grip. Surely the sight of such hands alone would attract any girl's notice. If not, then the tone of his hypnotic murmur would lure her. And if all else failed, which Mattie could not conceive of, then a look into Lord Westbury's keenly etched face would do the trick.

Mattie saw the way the horses tossed their heads, and William's correspondingly firm grasp upon the reins. His hands seemed bigger and his shoulders even broader as he controlled them.

Pamela was shy of him, but so eager to drive the carriage that she seemed hardly to notice his charm. William cautioned her once more as he adjusted one more loop between her fingers. He did not relinquish control entirely even when Pamela was ready, but placed his hands lightly over hers in case she should have need of him.

He gave the word, and Gerald jumped back onto the seat beside Mattie, stretching to see in front. Unused to a light open carriage, Mattie gripped the seat, expecting a lunge at the very least. But Pamela managed to ease the horses out fairly smoothly.

"Well done!" Gerald called. He was sitting so

far forward that Mattie thought he might spill onto the two in front. "Have her tighten up on that leader, Will."

William made the adjustment without responding. After they walked the length of the drive, he encouraged Pamela to take the team out onto the road and trot them.

Her movement must have been too abrupt, for one of the leaders bolted. Mattie felt a sharp jerk backward, but she recovered in time to see Pamela bringing the team back under control.

Instead of making a grab for the reins, William had calmly instructed Pamela how to do it herself.

"You shouldn't have had her trot them so soon, Will," Gerald grumbled. "You should have demonstrated longer than you did."

Mattie had to agree, but she could see that Pamela was thrilled to have stopped the horses on her own. Nothing daunted, she was eager to let them out again.

"Let me show her first, Will." Gerald bounced on the backseat.

"Gerald," William called patiently over his shoulder. "If you do not stop driving from the rear bench, I shall have to put you out."

Pamela giggled, and Gerald turned a mottled color.

"Just trying to help," he muttered, falling back against the seat.

"You are helping, and you shall help again," William replied, "but you might try entertaining the duchess while awaiting your turn."

Gerald started guiltily, and Mattie hid a smile.

He was an engaging boy, and she did not want to be a burden to him. Gerald had neither his brother's looks nor his Town polish, but his boyish enthusiasm pleased her.

To put him at his ease, she said, "I would be very grateful if you would explain some of the terms you and Lord Westbury are using. I am very ignorant, you see, when it comes to driving."

He brightened at a task he could so easily fulfill. "Certainly, Your Grace. Well, the two horses in front are called the leaders, naturally, and the two in back are known as wheelers. Each nag is guided by a set of ribbons—which is what we call the reins."

Seeing that Mattie had followed his very basic introduction, Gerald continued, "Did you see how Will made Lady Pam lace the ribbons through her fingers?"

She nodded.

"Well, it is done that way, you see, so one won't get them tangled up, and each horse may be controlled separately."

Gerald went on, and Mattie lent him half an ear while she strained to listen to the conversation taking place between her daughter and William. She half feared that Lord Westbury had set his brother the task of distracting her so that he could sweep Pammy off her feet when her mother was not watching. But, for the moment at least, she heard nothing to confirm her suspicions.

William took back the reins, and immediately Gerald's attention shifted forward.

"Is it my turn, Will?" he asked eagerly.

"In a moment."

William showed Pamela how to turn the carriage in a tight spot in the road. Then he addressed the proper way to hold the whip.

He gave a flick to his leader's ear, and the phaeton bounded forward, just as William trapped the thong in his fist.

To Mattie, the quick movement seemed a miracle of precision, so she was surprised when Gerald said, "What's got into you, Will? I've never seen you make such a mess of it."

"Thank you, Gerald. If I had known that you meant to point out my faults to the ladies, I should have had second thoughts about bringing you along."

Lord Westbury's teasing note robbed the words of their sting, and Gerald laughed. But Mattie was confused.

"I must say," she confessed to Gerald in a low whisper, "that I failed to see that your brother did anything amiss."

Gerald hovered anxiously over William's head as he attempted the maneuver again. "It's not that he did anything wrong, but I've never seen Will startle his horses so."

Lord Westbury tried the flick of the ear again, but his horses jerked forward as if they had shied.

"Will!" Gerald's voice was plaintive. "You shouldn't be teaching Lady Pam to do it the wrong way."

"Then perhaps you would like to show her yourself," William said over his shoulder. "I seem to be missing the knack today."

Gerald eagerly agreed, and as soon as William

brought the team to a halt, leapt out of the seat to go to the horses' heads. William trusted Pamela to hold the reins while the exchange of drivers was quickly effected, then came around back and climbed in beside Mattie.

She found that William occupied considerably more of the bench than had Gerald. Whether his larger size was to blame, or something more mysterious, she could not tell, but she immediately felt his nearness in a burst of heat.

As Gerald drove, William met her gaze, and a deprecating smile lit his eyes before it touched his lips. "I am afraid that I have just been given my *congé*."

"No, not at all!" Mattie felt an absurd desire to defend him. "You taught Pammy beautifully, and I am certain she is most grateful."

William sighed. "You are too kind, duchess. It is always wounding to one's pride to be outshone by one's younger brother."

"You could not be outshone." The words escaped her before she thought.

An irrepressible grin lit up his face, and Mattie was conscious once again of a heat stealing over her. Why, oh, why, she thought, did this man make her so uncomfortable?

"Thank you, duchess. Or may I call you Mattie since we are neighbors, and everyone else seems to do so?"

His request took her off guard. She was not familiar with the way such matters were determined in society these days, but His Grace's household had always been a casual one. At least, where she was concerned.

Mattie knew her servants' familiarity must

appear quite odd to a man who had been raised by Lady Westbury, so she hastened to explain. "You will think that I have a shocking lack of authority where my servants are concerned, and I must admit that I have. I was raised by His Grace after my parents died in a boating incident. You may have noticed that my servants tend to coddle me, but they all raised me, you see. They never have stopped thinking of me as a child."

"I should think that your marriage would have made them notice you had matured, if nothing else did." William's tone was perfectly even, but the accompanying glance, which raked her figure lightly, disconcerted her.

Flustered, and feeling her pulse quicken in response, Mattie blurted, "His Grace hardly noticed me himself, so why should they?"

William's brows jerked together. A question hovered behind them, but he did not speak it aloud.

"What I meant," Mattie said, talking much too quickly, she knew, "was that His Grace did not concern himself with social niceties. We married with little fanfare and went back to living the way we had always done."

"Surely not entirely?"

His questions were making her uneasy. How could one explain to a man of the world the sort of life she had led? There had been one difference, of course, and that difference had led to Pamela's birth, but it had not disrupted their routine for long.

"Not . . . entirely, no. Of course not. But His

Grace was getting along in years, as you must know, and his habits were already fixed."

"I understood that he seldom traveled. I only saw him in London a few times, and never in the Lords."

"No, he did not care for society. He had a tight circle of friends whom he did visit, and we had a few card parties of our own. He was quite fond of whist."

At William's appalled expression, Mattie took herself up short.

"You must not think that I yearned for more," she said, unsettled by his evident interest. "I found I did not care for London myself, and I had my gardening."

"Yes." William's look became teasing. "The consuming passion we two share."

Mattie felt her lips pulling up at the corners. It was going to be very difficult to suppress Lord Westbury's impudence, if he did not regret it himself.

She was so engaged by their conversation, she scarcely noticed what was going on in front of her until Gerald called back to them, "I say, Will! Your Grace! See what Lady Pam can do."

Mattie was surprised to note that an easy camaraderie had already sprung up between the two young people. Pamela was no more used to driving with gentlemen than Mattie was, but she *was* used to horses, and this shared interest had given her something to talk about. She and Gerald had been chattering like two cooks over a stew.

Once Gerald had their attention, he gave Pamela the word to begin. She attempted William's trick with the whip, and managed to step up the horses' pace without making them spring.

At Mattie's side, William gave another despairing sigh. "Bested first by my brother, and then by my pupil. This has been a very trying day."

Mattie had to laugh. She knew he had meant to impress Pamela with his driving skill. As ignorant as she was, she knew at least that much about gentlemen. But for all his efforts, Pammy seemed to prefer Gerald as her teacher.

"You should never have brought your brother along," she told William pityingly. "Though I must say, I am glad you did. He is a delightful boy, and so good with horses."

William winced. "I can see that my reputation has suffered a blow. On a future lesson, I shall have to issue Gerald a challenge."

"Future lesson?" The butterflies in her stomach resumed their fluttering. "Are there to be more?"

William looked surprised. "You didn't think that Lady Pamela could learn how to drive in just one, did you? I am sorry if you did, but this is only the first of many. Even as capable as she is, she must have more if she is to be trusted with her own carriage."

"But do ladies ever drive themselves?"

"In London it is all the rage. She will be going to London, will she not, in the near future?"

"Yes." Mattie nodded, trying to hide her misery at the thought. Her ignorance on ladies' driving habits was as great as it was on any other stylish matter. How would she ever manage to stage Pammy's presentation ball?

"Have I said something to distress you, Mattie?"

She shook her head at William's kind tone. "No, of course not. I simply had not thought so far ahead."

Realizing that this might be a good opportunity to remind him of Pammy's age, she added, "Thoughts of Pamela's London days are quite premature."

"Are they?" William allowed his dubious tone to speak for him. "She must have begun to think of it, nevertheless."

"I do not think so." Mattie drew herself up. It was time to recall her purpose in accompanying them. "I see no point in filling her head with matters she is too young to consider. There will be time and enough for London when she is grown."

She turned and made a discreet sign behind Gerald's back, before confiding to William in a whisper, "You must have noticed how much the child she is. She is younger than your brother, after all."

"But girls tend to marry so much younger than boys. You did so yourself."

Fear for Pamela stung her like a whip to her heart. "Yes, but that was extraordinary. If I had not been His Grace's ward, I am certain I never should have married him."

William's quick frown, his eyes softening with concern, awoke her to what she had said, and she hastened to amend it. "What . . . I meant, of course, was that I probably would not have met him."

"Ahhhh. Is that what you meant."

William's tone was rhetorical, but even so, Mattie had to fight the urge to explain herself further.

Feeling vulnerable, whether on Pammy's account or her own, she decided that it was time to call a halt to today's lesson. She suggested a return to the house, and was relieved when William did not protest. He seemed so confident, so flexible, as if, no matter what twists came his way through life, he would be assured of winning.

Perhaps that was what flustered her about him, Mattie decided. That, and not really knowing what he was thinking. A secret gleam often seemed to lurk in his eyes; his smile was so unrevealing. At times she thought he was laughing at her, but perhaps he was only amused by something else.

Gerald and Pamela had been talking animatedly while Gerald negotiated the gate, but now he called back, "I say, Will. Lady Pam has had the capital notion of setting up a breeding stud. Could we take her to visit Haverhill's stables?"

"Might I go, Mattie?" Pamela asked.

Mattie heard the eagerness in her child's voice, and fear gripped her again. Had Pammy already fallen prey to William's charms?

"We could discuss it," Mattie said, hoping to delay her decision.

But William, turning to her with a questioning look, made this impossible. "I should be most happy to conduct Lady Pamela to Lord Haverhill's estate. If she is seriously giving thought to setting up her stud, she would benefit greatly by seeing it. Haverhill might be willing to part with one of his stud's offspring, and she could do much worse."

When he saw her reluctance, he added, "Gerald will go with us, of course. I don't suppose we could prevent him in any way short of shackling him to the barn."

Before Mattie could say anything to discourage him, Gerald embarked on a description of the stud's bloodlines, in which the names Eclipse, Herod, and the Darley Arabian figured prominently. "You absolutely must see it, Lady Pam."

Mattie could easily imagine the light that must be shining in Pamela's eyes. She could hear the excitement in her daughter's voice all too clearly.

As anxious as she was about Pamela's heart, Mattie could do nothing to stop this particular event. Her very hesitation had as good as committed them.

"Certainly she may go," Mattie said, but then she turned to face William and hoped she looked firm. "But if she goes, then, necessarily, so must I."

"I would not have it any other way," William replied, and she could almost believe the note of sincerity in his voice, which was absurd. He was lounging back against the bench, looking for all the world like the cat who'd got the cream.

"Pammy is far too young to be undertaking

such a project, and far, far too young to go on outings without me."

"As you say, Mattie." William smiled, and the power of his dark eyes fell upon her.

*Lord have mercy on my poor baby,* Mattie thought.

# Chapter Five

As anxious as she had been about the outing, Mattie was almost sorry to see it end. She had never felt so stimulated, and she began to think that taking the air in an open carriage must be as efficacious as the medical men always said it was.

Before the gentlemen departed, Lord Westbury named a prospective date for the outing to Haverhill Grange, saying that he would call to confirm it within the sennight. Reflecting on the potential danger to her daughter's heart, Mattie saw in this provision an opportunity to put him off.

Upon their return, as soon as Pamela had run up to her room to change, Mattie spoke to Barlow. In as discreet a manner as she could manage, she gave him to understand that Pamela must never receive Lord Westbury alone.

"I perfectly understand, Your Grace. You may trust me to see that the gentleman in question does nothing to disturb your serenity."

"Thank you, Barlow," Mattie responded, while conceding to herself that William already had. "I think he will soon take the hint. Don't you?"

"One can always hope, Your Grace." Barlow's

lugubrious tone discouraged her from believing anything of the kind. "Although—if you will forgive the presumption—I have noticed that his mother, Lady Westbury, is surprisingly impervious to the discreet inflections one tries to use to achieve such discouragement."

"Well, we shall hope that her son is less so."

"As you say, Your Grace."

Mattie watched him amble off, feeling that her daughter was under seige, and that she herself was the only able-bodied soldier left to defend her.

Mattie's worry was justified only a few days later when, once again, William appeared in her garden. As on the first occasion, Mattie was wearing one of her outmoded gowns.

Turner's speed with a needle had been seriously curtailed by the rheumatism in her joints, and none of the gowns Mattie had ordered were ready yet. This muslin had been dug from the very bottom of her bureau, but it was the only suitable clothing she could find. Its skirt was shorter than was fashionable, and it revealed a hint of calf above her stout boots.

William, polite as he was, gave no sign of noticing her outlandish garb, but Mattie was certain he must be comparing her to the ladies he knew in London.

"Good morning, duchess," he said, sweeping off his beaver. "I thought I might find you here. It is a glorious day for gardening, is it not?"

"So glorious, in fact, that I am astonished to see you here when you might be busy with your own projects." The tartness of her own reply surprised her, but it simply was not fair for him to catch her at a disadvantage again.

"Oh, you needn't fear for my projects. I was up with the larks."

Not waiting to be invited, he stretched himself out on the ground to watch her as he had done before.

"I tried the house, naturally, but your man informed me that neither you nor Lady Pamela was at home."

Mattie stabbed the earth with her spade. William was proving to be every bit as arrogant as his mother.

"I am afraid that he did so under my instructions," she informed him.

A look of comical dismay came over his face. "My most profound apologies if I have offended. I thought we were agreed that I should call to confirm the date of our outing."

Mattie flushed, painfully aware of being in the wrong. "I must have forgotten, but I told you before that I am seldom home to visitors."

"Do you not care for company, Mattie?"

She avoided his searching look. "I live retired, as you must have guessed. I suppose I prefer my solitude."

He raised his brows with interest. "And why is that?"

Mattie shifted uneasily, then attacked a weed with a vicious pull. "I live in the country because I do not like London."

"Is it the amusements there that you find lacking? Do you have an aversion to the opera or the theater? I assure you there are more serious pursuits."

Mattie frowned in an obvious attempt to squelch him. "I do not particularly care for society." She hoped this answer would put an end to his questions once and for all.

But William persisted on a note of pure scientific inquiry. "I wonder why."

At such dogged perseverance, Mattie felt her back was to the wall, and she defensively blurted out, "I was not well received."

Then, in an attempt to shake the pall that had quickly settled around her, she shrugged. "I suppose one would say that I did not take."

"You surprise me," William said. His grave tone prompted her to search his face, but he quickly added, "And it is a pity, for I suppose I shall never see you in Town."

Mattie stared at him.

"Or Lady Pamela," he appended.

"Oh . . ." Mattie spoke airily, trying not to show how the thought of meeting him in society had flustered her. "I daresay you will see us eventually. I want Pammy to have at least one season in London."

"Do you? And why, may I ask?"

"Because I am determined that she shall enjoy herself amongst the ton."

"Even though you did not? How curious."

Mattie drew in a patient breath. Her breasts rose an inch above her décolletage, before she remembered how tight her dress was and exhaled quickly.

"Lord Westbury, you must know that I am a widow! I am not supposed to amuse myself!"

It was his turn to be surprised. "But I thought your bereavement occurred many years ago.

Ten—if I am not mistaken. I should think that even the most severe critic could not expect you to mourn longer than that. But perhaps you are speaking of a different person. Did you marry a second time?"

"Certainly not! When His Grace died, I was far too old for marriage!"

"How old?" Lord Westbury asked this nonchalantly.

Mattie colored. "I was twenty-five," she said. Then, at once, she regretted answering him, for she knew he was certainly older than that and only now contemplating marriage for the first time. But Lord Westbury, it seemed, could be as relentless as his mother.

"Not too old to remarry," he said, smiling gently.

Mattie felt her heart give a tremor.

Oh dear! she thought. If he smiles like that at Pammy, how will she ever resist him?

To hide these thoughts, she returned to her work and refused to respond to his comment.

William stayed seated, his forearms resting upon his knees. Mattie wondered how much longer he would insist upon waiting for Pamela. If she kept silent, she decided, perhaps he would go away.

"So you have been happy here at Westbury Manor?" he asked eventually.

"Yes, I always admired this site for a garden when I was a child."

"Then you perceived that it had promise. It is much more beautiful than I remembered it."

Mattie bit her lip. She ought not to have

started talking about the property; she could see how much it interested him.

"Yes, His Grace knew that *I* wished to live here," she said, hoping her tone would discourage him. "That is why he bequeathed it to Pamela."

"His Grace?"

She looked questioningly at him.

William smiled. "It just seems strange. You've referred to him several times that way. Instead of the usual ways, you know—Upavon . . . the duke . . . my husband. I presume he had a Christian name as well?"

The color rose to Mattie's cheeks. "Yes. Of course, I meant my husband. *His Grace* was simply what everyone called him. When I first came to live with him as a child, I thought that was his Christian name and always used it as such. No one bothered to correct me, and so . . . it lingered." She looked up to find William frowning, his keen gaze trained upon her face.

She stammered, "I heard the servants calling him that, you see."

"Yes." The frown was still on his face, making him look rather forbidding. "And how old were you when you married, Mattie?"

Mattie flushed again and looked away. "I was sixteen."

William said nothing more on the subject. After a while, he began to ask her questions about the garden and what more she planned to do with it. Mattie thought she ought to resent the questions, suspecting, as she did, his interest in Pamela's dowry, but at least they were less personal than his earlier ones.

Before she knew it, she found herself relaxing and even laughing from time to time as he showed his complete ignorance of horticulture. She wondered how he had ever had the nerve to tell such a bouncer about his roses!

When she had finished her work for the morning, he helped her to her feet once again, politely ignoring her soiled gloves. Feeling his gaze upon her, she removed one glove and self-consciously smoothed some of the tendrils of hair back from her face. She knew she looked a fright.

"Here, let me," he offered.

For a moment Mattie thought he meant to arrange her hair, and she retreated from him. But he immediately said, "Hold still."

So much authority rang in his voice that she found herself obeying him, and in the next moment he had extracted a small twig from among the strands.

"There." He handed it to her with a bow as if it had been a posy, and feeling curiously light-headed, she thanked him with a laugh before bidding him good day.

On the day of the outing to Haverhill Grange, Lady Westbury bestirred herself rather earlier than usual. She wanted to make certain of speaking to William before he set out.

She caught him just before he left the house and silently approved his appearance. His drab riding breeches fit him to perfection, as did the cut of an olive green coat. She was grateful to have one thing, at least, not to worry about, in that William always looked well turned out.

But when she noted that Gerald would be accompanying him again, she remarked irritably, "I am surprised, Westbury, to find you so lacking in forethought. It is not at all the thing to be taking one's younger brother along when one is courting."

The look William gave her was so bland that she wondered what he was thinking, but then a hint of humor lit his eyes and unsettled her.

"I appreciate the forcefulness of your argument, Mama, but I had to include Gerald on this occasion because it was he who proposed the outing."

Lady Westbury relaxed. "Well, I daresay he did it to advance your interests. I am happy to see that one of my sons at least shows a modicum of sense."

Gerald chose that precise moment to join them and greeted his mother with a dutiful peck upon one cheek.

Lady Westbury accepted this salute unconsciously, while saying, "You must do what you can to occupy the duchess, Gerald. I know it will be trying for you, but you're a good boy and you know your duty to the family."

William interceded for his brother, who seemed confused by her instructions. "Never fear, Mama. You may trust Gerald to do exactly what is needed in this situation."

They took their leave soon after that, so Lady Westbury had nothing to do but see them out with a care to be on their best behavior. A niggling worry did have her wondering why William had turned so complacent about her plans for him, but she told herself that her constant reminders of his duty as heir had finally paid off.

It would be surprising, indeed, she said to herself, if, after years of her governorship, he had not formed some notion of what was due to the Nortons.

Lady Westbury would have been greatly annoyed later to discover that William had ceded Gerald the driver's seat once again and had placed himself in the rear of the phaeton next to Mattie.

This surprised Mattie herself, but she reasoned that as the day trip had been concocted by Pamela and Gerald together, Lord Westbury could not very well edge his brother aside. And, she suspected, this would be an opportunity for William to try his hand at bringing her around.

Hoping to avoid any more embarrassing questions about her own marriage, she directed the conversation onto safer ground. Her complete ignorance of racehorses afforded her an opening topic.

"You say that Lord Haverhill runs an exemplary stable?" she asked, as Gerald urged the horses to a trot. "What does such an endeavor entail?"

"It entails a considerable expenditure for one, as Lady Pamela should be made aware before she embarks upon her own program. The horses themselves are dear, and at any time one might be injured and rendered worthless. Then the care for each runs to fifty pounds per year."

"Good gracious! Why?"

"Every racing horse must have its own stall and groom, as you will see today. It must be fed almost entirely on a diet of oats after the age of three. But these are minor costs to the threat that any one of them might turn out to be a failure and bring less than the cost of a year's feed when sold."

"Why would any sane person indulge in such a gamble?"

William smiled. "Ask your daughter or Gerald. This is their excursion, not mine."

Mattie knew what he meant without needing to hear the spirited conversation going on in the front seat. Pammy must have her horses, as Gerald must, too, she supposed, just as she herself must have her gardening, no matter what the sense of it. The thought that William had already discerned this about her daughter at once comforted and dismayed her. It meant that he would know how to lure Pammy all the more surely, but at least, if he did win her, then he would know how to make her happy.

A thought occurred to Mattie, and she gave voice to it at once. "Then you are not so passionate about horses yourself?"

A spark of humor lit his eyes. "I must confess to a greater interest in horses than I have in roses. But no, I am not so much the enthusiast that I want to set up my stud."

"What interests you, then?"

He shrugged. "Oh, a variety of things. I prefer not to be too tied, is all. The true enthusiast has no time for anything outside his principal passion, while I enjoy too many amusements to limit myself to one. I prefer to enjoy the fruits of an expert's labor to becoming one myself."

"I see. Then what do you do with your time?"

He cut her a sideways glance, but a teasing

note robbed his words of offense. "Unlike you, duchess, I do like society in all its absurdity. I enjoy the balls, the opera, and the theater. I go to my club and to the race meetings, or wherever my friends gather, whether it be at Jackson's Boxing Saloon or a house party. If I were to become addicted to any one sport, I would have to forfeit the rest."

"Oh." Mattie uttered the syllable rather wistfully. She could see that William had much to occupy his time. A man like William, who was handsome, urbane, and athletic, would be welcome in many settings. He would be at ease in the society that had shunned her.

"What plays have you seen?" she asked suddenly. If there was one regret she had always had about living as she did, it would be that she had missed visiting the theater. The thought of seeing great actors on the stage had always fascinated her.

"Well . . ." William thought for a moment before indulging her with a description of Edmund Kean's Hamlet.

Mattie listened as raptly as she had at Miss Fotheringill's knee when Gilly had first read the play to her. "I should love to see *Hamlet*," she confessed.

She was instantly afraid that she had opened herself up to further comment on her seclusion, but instead, William embarked on a description of another play. From there, it was but half a step to describing a costume ball with Venetian masks.

William's description of the dancers had Mattie in stitches. She could not help wishing she had seen such a spectacle. She had a quick vision of William, dancing in a black domino—his dashing figure cutting a swath in a sea of fancy dress as he bent his talents upon seducing a lady—and a pleasurable thrill ran down her spine. She could imagine that he might have had more than one such adventure, and a pang of envy seized her for all that she had missed.

Then the thought of Pammy's losing her heart to such an experienced man gripped her stomach.

Why, she asked herself, why would he want to wed Pammy?

For he must be pursuing Pamela. She could see no other fathomable reason for his wasting his time with them. The fact that this morning he had paid no attention to the two perched in front was neither here nor there, for she could easily ascribe it to William's perfect manners.

He had set his sights on Pammy, and she must do what she could to stop him.

With that thought firmly in mind, she resolved to keep his attention away from her daughter for the rest of the day, and by the time they reached Haverhill Grange, she could congratulate herself on having succeeded thus far. William was an entertaining conversationalist. She never once had to grope for things to say or feign to laugh at his jokes. In fact, the trip passed so quickly that she was surprised to find they had arrived.

Haverhill Grange stood among the western Suffolk Downs within easy distance of Newmarket. To reach the house and stables, they drove between fields of rippling grain in which Suffolk punches worked, pulling wagons. On the hill above them, a group of young Thoroughbreds cavorted in a meadow lush with green grass.

The horses' mood seemed infectious. Mattie could not help but catch something of their liveliness when the sun shone so brightly, and a tickling breeze played with the ribbons of her bonnet. William's phaeton skimmed lightly over the road until a hidden rock made it skip suddenly, which sent Mattie flying. William caught her and restored her to her seat with such a flourish of gallantry that she laughed like a girl, discovering that she could not truly be sorry they had come.

Lord Haverhill greeted them with all the loud courtesy of a wealthy farmer. Which was what he was, Mattie decided, and not the Town buck she had feared. His ruddy features, gray hair, and touch of gruff honesty reminded her of His Grace's brother Cosmo, who had inherited the dukedom, and she soon felt as at ease as she could among strangers.

Their host offered her his arm, but Mattie, fearing this would be too great an opportunity for William to make headway with Pamela, quickly pointed out her daughter as the principal in the group.

"Pamela is the one who is thinking of setting up her stables and the one who could most benefit from your discourse. I am afraid such valuable attention would be quite wasted on me."

Lord Haverhill politely dismissed her protest, but he soon recognized the aficionados among them. He could not fail to do so when Pamela fell into raptures over everything she saw.

Although Mattie had contrived the arrangement in some measure, it felt quite natural for William to fall into step beside her. She soon found herself on his arm, and could concede that he hid his disappointment very well. Their conversation in the carriage had done much to lessen the resentment she had begun to feel in his presence, so much so that she began to suspect him of trying his best to lull her into a false sense of security.

None of the arrogance she had witnessed in him appeared this morning; the stark lines of his countenance were relaxed. The gleam of humor so often in his eyes had lost its cynical edge, giving him a more open air.

It was as if the breeze had blown away his worldliness, the way her laughter had stripped her of years.

As they drew near the stables, Gerald launched into a description of Westbury Manor and its pasturage. Lord Haverhill listened with his farmer's ear and gave Pamela his best advice concerning the placement of meadows for yearlings.

Then they entered the stone building with its arched roofs and painted wooden stalls, and even Mattie had to gasp.

Inside were only six stalls. But each was enormous, large enough to give a groom plenty of space in which to maneuver. Each was occupied by a splendid Thoroughbred—four stallions and two mares—each horse measuring well over fifteen hands.

Mattie, who was reasonably ignorant of horses, admired their glossy coats and well-brushed manes and tails. Pamela, who knew much more, was rendered speechless.

Gerald hung back and anxiously watched for Pamela's reactions. The thought of being able to help her set up such an establishment so excited him that he could barely contain himself. William had been right about Lady Pam. She was different from other girls, and the evidence of this was in her attentiveness now. Visions of her standing in the winner's circle at Newmarket flashed through Gerald's head.

Unlike her mother, Pamela had a reasonable notion of how much such a venture would cost. But her father had left her a large fortune—so much, in fact, that the dream was well within her reach.

Gerald, with an enthusiasm to match Pamela's own, had only needed one comment from her to whisk her into the world of racehorses. Now he could be pleased by the intelligence of her questions. Lord Haverhill must have been impressed, too, for he answered them at great length. Gerald felt a certain pride in his protégée, and when their host turned back to converse with William and the duchess, Gerald took the opportunity to take Pamela aside.

He drew her over to one stall, opened it, and, with the groom's permission, showed her the manner in which racehorses must be shod. Not in the least intimidated by the horse's vast size or nervousness, Pamela soothed it, then bent to examine its shoe for herself.

"Here, Lady Pam," Gerald said in a low aside. "You've got to take another peep at Haverhill's prime stud."

The horse in question was one they had glimpsed on the general tour of the stables, the stallion that had brought Haverhill his greatest number of wins. Gerald entered its box, dragging Pamela by the hand.

"See here," he said, releasing her to run his hands over the horse's withers. "These are the points of confirmation to look for."

As he showed her, drawing special attention to the stallion's neck, withers, and haunches, Pamela followed his motions intently. The stallion was spirited, and at first, shied from a stranger, but Pamela got him to relax. Very soon, and to the groom's evident satisfaction, she had the horse both figuratively and literally eating out of her hands.

On the way out, Gerald and Pamela discussed horses and bloodlines as they trailed behind Mattie and Lord Westbury. Gerald was as excited as she was by her plans.

"I would be happy to advise you as you go along," he offered. Then, feeling the color stealing up his neck, he stammered, "If you wouldn't mind the interference, that is."

"Not at all," she insisted. "I'm not sure that I would know how to do it without you." It was Pamela's turn to blush. "Stocker never has wanted to help me, you see, but it seems as if you've given this much more thought than I ever have."

"I suppose I have," he admitted, "though you mustn't think I ever hoped of having a stud of my own. Will's a capital sort of brother; I mean to say, he's very generous, but I could never afford such a thing on my allowance."

"Then maybe we could be partners," Pamela said, excitement lighting up her face. "You could help me set up the stables and purchase my first horse. And if you saw one you would like to invest in, then maybe we could go halvers."

"Yes, I could do that! And if he won . . ." Gerald did not need to say more, but he could already see the string of Thoroughbreds they would own.

While the two younger people had been chattering away, William had kept a subtle eye on them and was pleased with what he saw. Something had told him that Lady Pamela was just the sort of girl to interest Gerald, and he had the feeling they would become fast friends, if nothing more.

He had told himself that his offer to take them on this outing had as much to do with Gerald's welfare as it had with his own curiosity about the duchess. But he was no longer sure. Her unguarded comments, so naively given, had sparked a protective instinct in him; her wide-eyed innocence had stirred his loins. After his many years on the town, he would never have believed that a woman could enchant him the way this one did.

The reasons for her disapproval of his attentions to Pamela were becoming more apparent. It was clear that Mattie's own marriage had been less than ideal. No wonder that she wanted to protect her daughter from such an error, if her own life had been cut short at a similar age.

To think that a woman as beautiful and charming as she should have chosen the life of a hermit seemed the greatest waste possible to

William. How she would adorn the most spectacular ballroom! He could picture her in fine lawn dresses, silk pelisses with fur trim, and fetching bonnets with blue ribbons to bring out the color of her eyes.

A sudden desire to dress her himself seized him so strongly that, at first, he did not hear his host's next remark.

"I beg your pardon, Haverhill." William hastened to cover his silence. "I must have been gathering wool. What was that you said?"

"I was telling the duchess that as soon as I heard you four were coming, I took the liberty of ordering up a luncheon for us. The servants are setting it up on the lawn now, if you will be so good as to follow me."

William started to express the normal platitudes, but he was interrupted by Mattie's distressed voice.

"Oh, but we mustn't! My lord, you are too good, but we must not disturb your servants!"

"What's that?" Lord Haverhill cocked his grizzled head as if he had not heard aright.

William took Mattie's hand and folded it over his arm. "Nothing, Haverhill, other than the duchess's polite reluctance to inconvenience your household."

"Inconvenience my—" Haverhill glanced at Mattie's concerned expression and did his best to understand. "Disturb the servants, what?" He paused. "Ha! That's a good one, duchess! Capital joke, what? Inconvenience my servants."

Chuckling, he turned his back to lead them across the lawn where the picnic had been laid.

William strolled after him more slowly with Mattie on his arm.

"Lord Westbury," Mattie ventured in a whisper. "Why did Lord Haverhill think I was making a joke?"

William had suppressed his own tendency to laugh, and now he did nothing more than smile. "I suppose that the notion that his cook should not cook and his butler should not—buttle, if you will forgive the invention—struck him as humorous."

"Oh, but I did not mean— Oh, I think I see." Mattie was quiet for a moment before asking, "You mean that to serve us all luncheon will not be a particular burden to them?"

"I hardly think so. We do not mean to stay forever, after all, and surely when they were engaged, they had some anticipation of having to work."

Mattie had been watching his expression while he answered her, so now he let her see his smile. She flushed as he had expected she would, but smiled back.

"On occasion," he emphasized strongly, deciding to prolong the joke. "We should not make a practice of coming every day or I suspect they might become disaffected."

"Then we shall take care not to abuse them, and I shall cancel all the plans I had made to move right in."

William was glad to see the twinkle in her eyes that told him she could enjoy some teasing. Again, that urge to take care of her, to bring out the dimples in her cheeks, and to touch her struck him strongly, making him wonder at himself.

This is no casual interest, he realized, knowing he had never felt precisely this way before. Of a sudden, his willingness to put himself out for Pamela made perfect sense. But William would bide his time, so he could watch this incomparable flower unfold before him.

# *Chapter Six*

$O$n a morning soon after, confused by yet another visit from William, Mattie decided to lay the problem at her best adviser's feet.

She found Miss Fotheringill seated by a window in the morning room, where she had repaired to do her mending. At the sound of Mattie's arrival, Gilly raised her head and greeted her, looking her over with approval. "I see that Turner has at last furnished you with something more decent to wear in the garden. This is much better, do you not think?"

Mattie looked down at her practical garment, a sort of cross between a walking gown and a dairymaid's pinafore, and sighed. "I suppose it is more decent. But I cannot help thinking that Marie Antoinette would have worn something just this absurd while pretending to be a peasant."

Gilly's eyes danced, but she answered quite soberly, "If Her Majesty of France wore such a garment, then it must be *comme il faut*."

"I suppose you are right."

Mattie's listless response raised a spark of concern on Gilly's face. "Is there something the matter, Your Grace?"

Mattie took the chair across from her and brushed the errant strands of hair away from her eyes. "It is only that Lord Westbury called again this morning, despite all my attempts to discourage him."

"Oh, dear. Do you mean that he continues to call for Pamela?"

Mattie nodded, then raised both hands in a hopeless gesture. "Barlow seems quite unable to discourage him. I have tried my best, but even though I make it clear that Pamela may not receive morning visitors, he insists upon coming around."

Gilly's brow rose. "Does he insist upon seeing her?"

"Oh, no. It is done so casually, you see. He rarely does more than ask after her health, so that I cannot, in all fairness, object. If he were more direct, I could send him about his business, but as it is, he pretends that his is nothing more than a neighborly visit. He stops on his morning ride to see how we get on, although he always troubles himself to stable his horse and find me in the garden."

"I see what you mean." Gilly took up her stitching again. "It is all quite unexceptionable."

"Yes," Mattie said miserably. "And he has been so kind—teaching Pammy how to drive and taking us on that truly delightful outing—you must see my dilemma."

Gilly pondered, and then asked, "Are you quite certain he *is* calling to see Pamela?"

"He must be! Why else would a gentleman who, according to all repute, seldom lingers in the country be spending so much time here? *We* might not regard it, but the social season is hardly more than half over. I can scarcely imagine all the functions he must be missing. And don't forget, his mother made it quite clear that Pamela was the object of their first call."

She sighed again. "It must be her dowry he wants, although I should think Lord Westbury would be reasonably well off without it. But, perhaps—living in Town the way he does— Oh, Gilly! You don't think he has gambling debts, do you?"

"I shouldn't think so, but it is possible. I can see why you would be concerned, but I have never seen any sign that Pamela—" Gilly broke off. She pondered for a moment before giving her head a little shake.

"What?" Mattie rose straight up in her chair, alarm on her face. "What have you noticed?"

Gilly's glance was cautious. "I was going to say that I had not seen any signs of infatuation, but I must confess that she has been a bit distracted of late. I was attributing it to this scheme of hers for setting up her stud, but it could be that she is feeling something else."

Mattie clapped both hands to her face. "It is exactly what I feared."

"Not necessarily. Who knows what dreams will make a girl's eyes shine?"

Mattie groaned. "You have not seen him. If you had, you would not need to ask."

She fell silent, staring at the wall for a time, before saying in a desperate tone of voice, "Gilly, what can I do? How can I make him leave my Pammy alone?"

"Would he be so bad a husband for her?"

"No, it's not that. But she's a baby. And even if she weren't, I still would want her to meet scores of men and take her pick from them. If I thought that Lord Westbury were in love, it might be different, but when she's with him, he gives no sign of feeling that way."

Gilly studied her. Then she asked softly, "Would you know how to tell if he was?"

Mattie stammered, "I . . . You are thinking, of course, that I would not recognize the signs, and perhaps you are right. All I can say is that he makes little attempt to keep her attention, and I should think—" She faltered, then continued more firmly, "I want her to marry someone who cannot be happy without her."

"Well, then—" Gilly straightened her shoulders "—we must do what we can to make him realize that she is much too young to make him happy."

"Fine. But how?"

"You must make him feel the difference in their ages. Perhaps it has been wrong to keep them apart, when, if he spent any time with her, he would see at once that they are not suited for each other. From all you say of Lord Westbury, I would suspect him to be a man of sophisticated tastes, whereas Pamela only thinks of her stables."

"You mean, let him call on her?"

"Yes, in measure. And I should be there as chaperon. I cannot think that his lordship will find it entertaining to be calling on a schoolgirl and her governess, not when compared to the pleasures of Town."

Mattie considered, and a hint of hope lightened her tone. "You could be right."

"Yes, I believe I am. Then, you might think of something else, some manner of bringing home to him, as nothing else would, the difference in their ages."

"Like what?" Mattie listened eagerly.

"Like . . ." Gilly paused. "Like giving a rout."

"A rout!" Mattie squeaked. "Me?"

"Yes." Gilly spoke more confidently now. "A man of Lord Westbury's experience should find it quite flat to be engaged for a children's party. When he sees how tame the amusements are—and especially how tame the refreshments—that should cure him of his intent."

"But how would I ever go about doing such a thing?"

"I will help you. I remember some of the parties my first employer gave for her children. Many years ago, of course, but I doubt that children's amusements have changed much since that time." Gilly laughed, then added with a touch of deviousness, "We shall serve nothing but lemonade and orgeat."

"But who would come? I don't know anyone."

"You could invite the young people in the neighborhood. I daresay Mrs. Puckeridge could help you with a list."

Mattie's cheeks had paled with the first mention of a party, and now she spoke in a tone of panic. "She would probably love such a thing. But I don't know. Do you think we could manage it? What if no one came? What if they all came and were bored?"

Gilly looked at her firmly. "You are a duchess, my dear. Of course people will come, and young people are never bored when they are placed in a room all together."

"They're not?" Mattie looked up at her and flushed. "I suppose you are right, but since I never . . ."

"You may take my word for it. The planning should be relatively easy. And this will be good practice for you before Pamela's presentation."

Mattie reflected unhappily for a moment. Then she conceded finally, "Yes, it would. It would be far better to get my feet wet here than in London."

"That's the spirit," Gilly said.

"But—" another thought had occurred to Mattie to cast her in the dumps "—it will never work. I could never persuade Barlow to help me. He will say the staff is not big enough."

"You must insist upon it. He can always hire extra help from the village, or perhaps some of your neighbors would be willing to lend a few of their servants for the evening."

"Do you think they would?"

"I should think that if you make it known that the Duchess of Upavon is having a rout, *and* intending to invite their sons and daughters, your neighbors will be only too glad to help."

Mattie took a shaky breath. "Yes, you're right, of course." She looked Gilly timidly in the eye and confessed, "It is simply that I never have felt much like a duchess."

"Yes, my dear, I know." Gilly rose and came over to place a warm hand upon Mattie's shoulder. "But you are a duchess, and for Pamela's sake, you must begin to act like one."

Mattie covered Gilly's hand with her own and nodded. "Yes. Once again, you are right."

Inhaling deeply, she rose to her feet. "Very well. I shall give a rout. Now, what shall we do first? Do you suppose— Oh, dear!"

"Now what?"

"Do you think they will expect to dance? I have forgotten how, and Pamela never has been taught."

"Then it will be time to engage a dancing master. I shall inquire about one directly."

Mattie's blue eyes softened as she gazed upon her old governess. "Oh, Gilly. Where would I be without you?"

"You would do just as well without me, I daresay."

"No," Mattie said decisively. "I would not."

It was no more than a day later that Mrs. Puckeridge, the rector's wife, while scolding the kitchen maid for spoiling the perfectly good leg of mutton she had intended for dinner, heard the sound of carriage wheels upon the drive. Looking out a window, she was astonished to see the traveling coach of the Duchess of Upavon pulling up in front of the rectory. An ancient coachman unbent himself from the box, lowered himself slowly to the ground, and hobbled around to the carriage door.

He handed out not only Her Grace's companion—a woman who, Mrs. Puckeridge considered, acted far above her station in life—but also the duchess herself, dressed for a morning call.

In a sudden flurry, Mrs. Puckeridge dismissed

the kitchen maid, then frantically called her back and adjured her in a loud whisper to ready the tea tray and not to make a muck of things this time. That order given, she ran to a mirror to tidy her hair and smooth her dress, thinking all the while what a *coup* this was.

She knew for a fact that the Duchess of Upavon had neither originated calls nor returned those from her neighbors. Not even the calls from Lady Westbury herself. Mrs. Puckeridge had spent a cozy hour with her ladyship only the day before in which they had discussed Her Grace's deficiencies in this respect at length.

She knew that Lady Westbury would be particularly irked to discover that Her Grace had chosen one of her humbler neighbors on whom to confer this honor, and she could not wait to be the bearer of such tidings to her ladyship herself.

By the time the bell was pulled, she had composed herself in an attitude of virtuous leisure in her parlor, to appear as if she had been stitching there all morning. When the guests were ushered in, she could set down the altar cloth she was hemming and appear surprised.

"Your Grace." Mrs. Puckeridge swooped her the deep curtsy she had practiced for days on first learning of the duchess's arrival in the vicinity and had subsequently had so little occasion to use. She gave a chilly nod to Miss Fotheringill, who accepted the greeting with a gentle smile.

Mattie noticed the hint of amusement in Gilly's eyes and decided not to let Mrs. Puckeridge's obsequious behavior discommode her. They had come for a purpose, and she could not complain of her hostess's behavior when her own motives for calling were far from noble. She accepted the chair Mrs. Puckeridge offered and looked to Gilly to help her through the preliminaries.

Mattie had no practice in making small talk, and she had insisted that Gilly accompany her to help her with this part of her mission. She needn't have worried, for Mrs. Puckeridge, with her incurable nosiness, was quite capable of filling the void with impertinent questions of her own.

It was not long before she touched upon Lady Pamela, and wondered aloud why Her Grace had not thought to bring her daughter to meet one of her own, so that Mattie was soon able to jump in with her plans for the rout.

As soon as the rector's wife heard that the Duchess of Upavon would be eager to give a party for her daughter if she were not so woefully new to the neighborhood that she did not quite know where to begin, Mrs. Puckeridge leapt to offer her services.

Yes, she said delightedly, she would be more than happy to help with the guest list, and to prove her capability on that score, she gave a rapid, though incomplete, rundown of the neighboring families with children of a suitable age. She made a mental note to write her own son immediately and insist that he come down from Oxford to attend the rout.

When dancing was mentioned, she said she fancied Monsieur Le Gros, an *émigré* in the High Street, could be applied to for lessons in all the most up-to-date steps. And, she said, if Her

Grace would not be offended by the suggestion, she could recommend both a caterer, to supply excellent food and drink, as well as several girls—virtuous, hardworking girls—who might be taken on as extra servants if needed.

By the time Mattie left, accompanied by Gilly, Mrs. Puckeridge had solved all the most pressing details of the rout and Mattie could relax in part, knowing, at least, what steps she had to take next.

She left Mrs. Puckeridge up in the boughs, for that lady, after suffering a series of rebuffs at Her Grace's door, had begun to relinquish her long-cherished dream of becoming the duchess's primary confidante. Now, with one stroke, her ambition had been restored, and for several moments after her guests' departure, she could only stare at the door that had closed behind them with a smile upon her face.

Emerging from this glowing reverie, she suffered an immediate burst of dissatisfaction at finding herself alone. She knew that her morning would be quite ruined if she could not impart her bit of gossip to someone who, as a result of learning the extent of her involvement in the duchess's scheme, would be eaten up by envy.

Putting aside the plans for her morning's work, she took up her cloak and ordered up the gig to make a call on Lady Westbury.

Her ladyship's reaction to the news was not entirely what she'd anticipated, although for one brief, blessed moment, Mrs. Puckeridge could detect a touch of resentment in her ladyship's eyes. Then Lady Westbury recovered herself and assumed an expression of great secrecy and importance.

"This is no more than to be expected," her ladyship stated, folding her hands tidily in her lap. "Not but what I should have expected the duchess to call upon me if she had need of particular guidance in a social matter, which I daresay she must. However, considering the likely reason for her sudden decision to entertain, I can quite see why she hesitated to apply to me. The answer is entirely obvious."

"Oh?" Mrs. Puckeridge was finding herself once again on the out, which she could not like. But it would be just *like* Lady Westbury to attempt to undercut her accomplishment. "Is there some particular reason why she would hesitate to come to you for assistance?"

Lady Westbury smiled smugly. "I am not at liberty to say, but you must know that my son Westbury has been calling upon Lady Pamela. His attentions have been most assiduous over the past few weeks. He has been teaching her how to drive his phaeton—though why any gel would wish to know how to drive such a dangerous vehicle, I cannot imagine—and I know, besides, that she has applied to both my sons for advice concerning the use of her pasturage."

"I see. . . ." Mrs. Puckeridge said in a tone designed to invite confidence.

"I see that you do." Lady Westbury beamed upon her inferior with satisfaction. "It would be too early for me to speak openly, but I can congratulate myself on being the instigator of this particular match. It only took a hint from me for Westbury to see the advantages to himself and to his family. Westbury Manor, as you must know, from its name if from nothing else, once formed a part of his patrimony, and it has always seemed to me a crime that it should no longer be so. Since Lady Pamela had inherited, it seemed the perfect opportunity to replace it where it belongs."

"I see," Mrs. Puckeridge said again, but she wondered to herself if the duchess did see. She filed away this bit of knowledge as something that might be useful at a later date. She could not believe that Her Grace of Upavon was aware of Lord Westbury's machinations, and as prime confidante, the post she now expected to obtain, she had a duty to watch out for her friend's interests.

Now that Lady Westbury, in spite of her best intentions, had let the cat out of the bag, she could not restrain herself from talking about the possibility of the match. It was not long either before her dissatisfaction with the duchess rose to the surface.

"She is a shatterbrain," Lady Westbury said, "so it is no wonder that poor Lady Pamela has been left to grow up quite wild. Not that I fault the child in the least! No, she is a charming gel— Westbury said so himself upon meeting her—and it will please me to have the governing of her. I almost begin to think it will be a love match. A mother notices these things, and I must say there is rather an unusual air about him—"

She gave herself a brisk shake and continued stiffly, "But I do not approve of such things, as I told Westbury myself. I am only content that he saw fit to heed my advice, for I have to admit that he has not always. And I have advised him not to let it worry him that the gel's mother is such an eccentric. The old duke was one, so it's to be expected that his relic would be."

Lady Westbury's nostrils flared with distaste. "Still, one cannot but wonder why she insists upon carrying on as if the polite world were not a fit place for her existence."

Mrs. Puckeridge allowed Lady Westbury to rattle on while she stored away her bits of gossip. Though her ladyship had denied her the full pleasure of imparting her news, she still had the satisfaction of learning the true state of affairs from Lady Westbury herself.

Who would have thought that a gentleman of Lord Westbury's stature would marry a girl over such a small parcel of land?

News of the Duchess of Upavon's rout swept through the neighborhood so rapidly that it was generally known—many bets on the likelihood of its really occurring had even been placed—long before the actual invitations were sent out.

William heard the news with interest. He received it almost simultaneously with discovering a change in Mattie's policy for receiving visitors.

He had made it his practice to call at the house before searching for Mattie in her garden. Barlow's attempts to dissuade him were so blatant that William had at once perceived their usefulness as a weathervane to gauge his progress, and he was gratified one morning to find that the door was no longer barred to him.

He had called alone and been subjected to a painful half hour of nursery chat, with Pamela's governess, Miss Fotheringill, in attendance. But after this one success, he made sure to take Gerald along and, following a scheme of his own, advanced the notion of Gerald's riding on a daily basis with Pamela.

Since he had contrived to make Gerald issue the invitation, and he himself had made no attempt to join in their party, neither Mattie nor Pamela's governess had raised the least objection. William had observed all this with a secret smile.

It was on a morning soon thereafter that he and Gerald called upon the ladies and interrupted them in the middle of a dancing lesson.

Barlow, a long-suffering expression upon his face, showed them into the small saloon, where the ladies were assembled. Miss Fotheringill was seated at the pianoforte, picking out the accompaniment to a country dance. An elderly Monsieur Le Gros, powdered and bewigged, the waist of his knee breeches held in by tight corseting, stood in the corner, clapping out a rhythm while Pamela and Mattie executed their steps.

William watched for a few moments in amusement as Mattie stiffly acted out the part of gentleman to Pamela's less-than-graceful lady. Then Monsieur Le Gros perceived the intruders and, with an exclamation of delight, informed the ladies that aid had arrived.

Mattie, who, at this precise moment, was executing a low bow that showed the delightful roundness of her hips, gave a squeak. As she spun to face William, one hand flew to cover her lips.

Pamela reddened under Gerald's wicked grin.

Miss Fotheringill stopped playing and nodded graciously to William's bow.

"But this is excellent!" Monsieur Le Gros was saying, nearly hopping with suppressed excitement. "If *Messieurs* would oblige, we could now form two couples to learn the more difficult steps, *n'est pas? Messieurs?*"

Gerald started backing toward the door through which they had come, his agitated stammer producing stream upon stream of apologies, but William quickly cut off his retreat.

"Where do you think you're going, you young jackanapes?" While the ladies gazed on in amused silence, he held on to the back of Gerald's collar, making his escape virtually impossible.

"For God's sake, Will! You don't expect me to dance, do you?" Gerald whispered fiercely. "I wouldn't know how to take the first step."

"You do not need to know how. That is the most remarkable thing about dancing lessons. The dancing master teaches you the steps."

"Aw, Will, you know what I mean. I'll make an ass of myself."

"No, you won't. Any sprig who can learn to drive and box and fence with the best of them can learn a few paltry dance steps."

"I am sure Gerald will do excellently." Mattie came forward to intervene. "But I would hate to coerce him into anything he would find repugnant."

"Gerald finds anything of a civilized nature to be repugnant," William replied. "However, if you would not object to our intrusion, this would be a prime opportunity to slap some polish on this barbarian."

Mattie laughed and took Gerald's arm, saying in a coaxing voice, "How could I object? We have all been learning, you see, for my own skills are very rusty indeed, and they are only now coming back to me. I promise to help you as we go along."

"Thank you, Mattie," William said, handing over his captive.

He smiled at her and saw her cheeks turn rosy under his regard. Her self-conscious response raised a heat deep inside him, which made it difficult to tear his eyes away. He turned toward Pamela and offered her his arm.

Now that there were two couples, he and Pamela could square off against the other two for the country dance, letting their imaginations and the intervening beats in the music fill in for the two missing sides. As the most practiced dancer of the group, William could perform his part without thinking and spent his time observing the others.

His own partner could not converse when all her attention was needed to govern her feet. Lady Pamela danced with her gaze fixed solidly on the floor in front, so that William was at leisure to peer at the other two.

He had to keep himself from laughing at the dejected air of his brother, who seemed to find dancing more difficult than all his considerable athletic pursuits put together. William would never have believed that his graceful Gerald could look so clumsy if he had not witnessed the scene himself.

Mattie, on the other hand, looked like the duchess she was in a flowing skirt that swirled when she walked, with her piquant little chin held high in the air. She danced as if the music flowed through her veins. Her happy expression as she turned and curtsied told William all he wanted to know.

He had to be careful not to stare at her, so he turned his eyes back to his partner and politely kept them there until it was his and Mattie's turn to execute a step together. When they did, and took a turn about the center of the square, his gaze found hers for one electric moment. The beat in his throat grew more rapid as she turned away in confusion. The feel of her fingertips in his—for neither wore gloves—set a current pulsing to his loins.

When that country dance was over, Monsieur Le Gros clapped his hands in delight.

"That was far more better, *messieurs et mesdames. Messieurs*, I cannot thank you enough."

"It was our pleasure," William responded. Then, before he and Gerald could be dismissed, he added, "But the ladies surely must learn more. While we are here, perhaps it would be wise to practice the basic steps of a Sir Roger de Coverley, for that cannot be danced without couples to exchange."

Monsieur Le Gros became his ally, taking him up on his offer despite Gerald's frown. The couples arranged themselves with Gerald at his left and the ladies facing them from an imaginary line.

Miss Fotheringill found a suitable sheet of music, a lively piece written in six-eight time, so they had a vigorous accompaniment. Without any other couples to support them, the ladies switched partners back and forth, going rapidly from William to Gerald, faster and faster, until even Gerald was laughing at the absurdity of it.

When everyone was breathing heavily from exertion, and Mattie had ended up his partner, William called a sudden halt.

"We must save some of our energy for the waltz," he said.

Mattie's eyes grew round. Cornflower blue stared back at him before she said, "You do not mean to teach us to waltz?"

"But of course. Why not? It is danced everywhere now, except at Bath, and I know you would not wish for Pamela to appear to disadvantage." He knew he was using Pamela shamefully, but he did not intend to leave Mattie's house without feeling her once in his arms.

"Oh, no!" Mattie responded precisely as he had expected. "She must never appear to be a country bumpkin! That would not do at all!"

The distress in her voice made William wince with guilt. He had already guessed that there must have been some episode in her past to make her so uncomfortable with society. Nothing he had seen had convinced him that she had a natural aversion to entertainment.

Her fascination with the theater was so palpable that he could almost feel her disappointment at the performances she had missed. Today alone, he had watched her dance and seen how much she would enjoy a ball. Something, or someone, he decided, had done something to spoil society for Mattie.

Vowing to himself to make it up to her, he started to take her in his arms, but she pulled back in confusion.

"Oh, but I couldn't!" she protested breathlessly. "I don't know how to waltz!"

William gave her a teasing grin. "As I have already told Gerald, the most remarkable thing about dancing lessons is that one doesn't need to know the steps. I am sure Monsieur Le Gros will teach them to you, but if he will not, I will."

While she was laughing in response, he took her into his arms, and they stayed in that agreeable position while Monsieur Le Gros showed Gerald how to tame Pamela.

# Chapter Seven

*W*hile they waited, in order to keep Mattie from drawing away from him, William began to show her the basic steps.

"You must keep your feet always on the floor," he said before starting his count. "The object is to glide about the floor with your partner as your guide."

"Which partner?" Mattie looked up at him shyly.

The sight of those blue eyes so close to his dulled his wits for a moment. "I beg your pardon?" William said.

"Which partner is to do the guiding? You or me?"

"Ahhhh." William nodded and smiled to himself.

Having never seen the waltz, Mattie naturally had never learned its conventions, which were unlike any other dance.

"I see the source of your confusion. The privilege of leading, however, is strictly the male's, and I am afraid that my feelings will be gravely injured if you do not follow me."

Mattie dimpled. She still looked flustered by the unaccustomed contact. The roses in her cheeks were in full bloom, and her blush extended down to her décolletage, which was unfashionably low.

William could only be grateful for the peculiar circumstances that kept her gowned as she was rather than in the current, more modest mode. He suspected that Mattie was either too softhearted to demand more dresses from her aged dresser or too timid to hire a younger woman to do the work. The result of her inexperience spurred his senses. He would be sorry to have it rectified, though he knew it soon would be.

He cleared his throat and began his lesson, dropping his gaze to the floor between them. "We will be moving to the count of three. Please do not be either offended or alarmed if I push you backward, for that is how the dance is done."

He moved slowly against her before Mattie hastened backward to avoid brushing his limbs. She fixed her eyes to the floor, and William watched her steps until she had mastered the movements. Once that was accomplished, his gaze was free to roam at will.

Golden streaks sparkled through her hair, which shone like satin. Although his mother would not have approved Mattie's long hours in the sun, they had left only a radiant glow to her cheeks.

If he had met her in any other place, he would have been drawn to her, but William could only be thankful he had found her untouched as she was.

A sound intruded upon his thoughts, but it was a moment before he realized that Monsieur Le Gros was attempting to claim their attention.

They had been so intent, she on her steps and he on her, they had not noticed.

"The music, please, Miss Fotheringill."

Gerald and Pamela had squared off like two boxers in a clench, their heads firmly directed to the floor between them. William stifled a laugh, though the sight of these two determined horsemen in a ballroom would be enough to send his mother into a spasm of nerves.

The music started, and he and Mattie waltzed about the room. She had a gift for dancing. Only her shyness kept her gaze to the floor, for he was sure the steps did not.

"It is thought a useful practice to converse with one's partner while simultaneously keeping up the steps. Shall we try it?"

She dimpled rosily again as she dared to glance upward. "I am perfectly willing, but I cannot speak for my feet. If they tread on yours, you must blame them and not me."

"Agreed. It will be infinitely worth it to see your face instead of the top of your head . . . charming though that is," he hastened to assure her.

"Lord Westbury—" Mattie chuckled and shook her head "—I am sure you are what Gerald would call 'a most complete hand.' With you as my partner, I shall learn everything, right down to the ballroom flattery."

"You wound me, duchess. There is no need for flattery in present company. My compliment was sincere, but if Gerald has been saying anything behind my back to ruin my reputation, I shall have to speak to him firmly."

"Gerald would be far too well mannered to do

anything of the kind, and besides, he seems to be sincerely attached to you."

William felt a warm smile stealing across his features. "And I to him, in spite of his social shortcomings."

They both glanced Gerald's way at that moment and discovered the younger couple bounding about the room. Monsieur Le Gros was holding his hands to his head in despair.

"Gerald," William called, bringing his own steps to a halt, "this should be a glide, not a fandango."

"What's the difference?" Gerald shrugged and glanced backward, nearly careening into a chair.

Mattie suppressed a giggle, and William winced visibly for her benefit. "I might have known you would say something to put me to the blush."

"That's poppycock." Gerald kept right on with his bounding, and Lady Pamela laughed riotously as they twirled about the room. "Lady Pam and I are happy enough, and that's what counts."

"Well said, sprigling." William caught Mattie's eye and smiled at her understanding look. "At least he knows that pleasing one's partner is of the greatest importance."

A hint of sadness flickered in her eyes, which confused, then dismayed, him. "You are kind to think that way," she said.

William felt the muscles in his jaw twitch. He could not respond as he would like in front of everyone else, so instead he swept her into his arms and said, "Let's give Gerald's method a try, shall we?"

Without waiting for Mattie's reply, he spun her

in a wide circle until she was laughing, her head thrown back in delight. Monsieur Le Gros clapped his hands in reprimand, and the prevailing atmosphere in the small saloon matched the utter chaos in William's heart.

When the lesson was over, and the gentlemen long departed, Mattie wandered about the small saloon in a deep reverie. She hummed the tune of the waltz, and every now and then executed a dipping step to the beat.

Soon Gilly joined her and saw her waltzing by herself. She paused at the door and a frown of concern descended on her brow.

"Are you alone, Your Grace?"

Mattie spun and gave a startled laugh. "Oh, yes," she stammered. "I must appear quite ridiculous, which makes it good it was you who discovered me and not Barlow. I should never keep his respect if he caught me out in such a foolish posture."

Gilly smiled, but her brow remained furrowed. "You enjoyed the dancing?"

"Yes. It was quite delightful. I had not realized how much fun it could be."

Sadness hovered on Mattie's features, and a sudden pang smote Gilly's heart. "I think that Pamela enjoyed it, too," she said, to redirect the subject.

Mattie laughed. "Of course she did. It is just the sort of romp that would please her. And Gerald was so charming, was he not? He is such a dear boy."

Her smile faded then. Gilly could see that she was troubled.

"Is there anything else you wish to tell me?"

Mattie's eyes flew to hers. "Yes, Gilly. I have been thinking about Wil ... about Lord Westbury."

She stumbled over his name, and again Gilly's heart felt a stab of worry. She had watched them dance, had seen his lordship's smooth performance and Mattie's glow, and a frightening possibility had leapt into her mind.

"What about his lordship, my dear?"

"It's—about Pamela." Mattie wrung her hands. "Oh, Gilly, what if I've been wrong? What if he would make the perfect husband for Pammy?"

Gilly hid her surprise as a measure of relief filled her chest. "What made you change your mind so suddenly?"

"I can't be sure. It may not even be changed. But I cannot help thinking—" Mattie took an agitated tour about the room and came to a halt beside Gilly. "He is so gentle, you see. So kind and considerate. To hear him speak—he spoke of making one's partner happy—which convinced me, you see, that he would be a thoughtful husband. The way he taught me how to waltz—I could tell that everything he said was meant to put me at ease. Which it did! Oh, Gilly, surely a man like that would make the greatest husband for any girl."

The seed of worry was growing stronger now and making Gilly feel weak at the knees. She could not bear to see her favorite's heart broken, which it would be if Mattie ever perceived that she'd fallen in love.

"If what you say is true—" Gilly thought rapidly "—then yes, I can see why you would want

Pamela to consider him. His age is not so much greater than hers that she would be unhappy as his wife."

A look of relief lightened Mattie's features, though the touch of sadness still remained. "It is so hard to know what is best."

Gilly put an arm about her. "True. We cannot always know. But if you think Lord Westbury might, after all, be a proper candidate for Pamela's hand, then perhaps you should not put yourself so much in his way. You should let me act as their chaperon and give them time to know each other better."

"Of course, that would be the right thing to do."

Gilly thought, If it would be so right, then why does Mattie look sad at the mention of seeing him less?

She hoped she had made the most constructive suggestion under the circumstances. She still believed Lord Westbury to be the wrong man for Pamela, but it was clear that Mattie should spend less time in his hypnotic company.

Her heart had never been touched before, never been given a chance to bloom as other girls' had. Gilly did not want to see it open, only to be crushed by unrequited feelings. Lord Westbury was her junior by many years, and whatever his intent, it was not likely to be directed toward Mattie.

"Then you may leave his lordship to me," Gilly said, "and not give him a second thought."

Plans for the rout continued, and soon Mattie was surprised to find herself caught up in the excitement. Now that Lord Westbury had been admitted to the house, he often found the time to call, and had offered his help as well. This made it difficult for Mattie to leave him entirely to Gilly, as Gilly had suggested, for she had no sooner mentioned in William's hearing the need to engage extra servants for the party than girls from the village began showing up on her doorstep. Soon thereafter, a caterer knocked on the door, giving, by way of introduction, a recommendation from his lordship.

Before she quite knew how it had happened, Mattie had started saving all her most pressing questions for William. If he did not always know the answer, he did know the quickest way to find it out. When asked, he could tell her what games had been played at the most fashionable London parties this season, which dances would be most proper to play for a group this age, or how many decorations would be needed in the saloon.

Under his tutelage, Mattie began to think that her rout would be as fashionable as any in London.

Caught up in the novel issues of entertainments and refreshments, Mattie forgot until the last moment to order herself a new gown. She might not have remembered this at all if William had not broached the subject himself.

They were sitting in the morning room. William, as he had several times before, had made the mistake of calling when Pamela and Gerald were on their ride. Mattie had invited him to wait until the others returned, knowing how disappointed he would be to miss seeing Pamela.

When the subject of the rout was raised, he desired to know what colors she and Pamela would be wearing so that he and Gerald might send flowers to match their gowns.

His request threw Mattie into a fluster, which was heightened even more by the rush of pleasure she instantly felt.

No other man had ever offered to send her flowers, especially not flowers to match her gown. Mattie was groping for a composed response when she suddenly remembered that she had made no plans at all for her wardrobe, and the confidence that had been slowly building inside her at the ease with which all the arrangements were being made exploded in a gasp.

"Our gowns! Oh, good Lord, I forgot all about them!"

William's lips began to twitch, and she could feel her cheeks burning with embarrassment. She had been so pleased with her own efficiency, and for William to see what a dunderhead she really was . . .

"If you have forgotten to pick them up from the modiste, I should be only too happy to fetch them for you. Just give me her address, and it will be done."

"You are most obliging—but I— It was very foolish of me, but—" His kind expression prompted her to confess, "I am afraid I forgot to order a new gown either for Pamela or for myself. I don't know how I could have been such a dolt."

"You are not a dolt, and I should not worry at all if I were you. There is still plenty of time for someone to make you up something new."

"But you don't understand! Turner—my dresser, that is—would find it impossible to sew that fast. Her joints are swollen, you see, and I could not ask that of her."

Mattie sighed, and tried to think which of her gowns could serve the purpose with perhaps a change of trimming or some new ribbons.

"Wouldn't it be possible," William suggested in a cautious tone, "to use the modiste in the village? She is quite good, from what my mother tells me. I don't know her name, but Mama could send you her card. I am certain she would be happy to do so."

"Oh! But I couldn't impose upon Lady Westbury." The thought alone made her tremble.

"Nonsense. It would increase her image enormously to have it known that the beautiful Duchess of Upavon and she use the same dressmaker. She would not hesitate for a minute to supply it."

"But I don't even know what I want." William was so kind to call her beautiful, she told herself to keep from blushing. He always showed such consideration of ladies' feelings.

William spoke in a patient voice, but his eyes danced. "I am not that familiar with the process of ordering feminine apparel, but from what I understand, the modiste will have pictures to choose from. She can advise you on the latest styles, and the most suitable colors."

"Really?" Mattie began, almost, to feel hopeful. If ordering drinks and hors d'oeuvres had been as easy as she had found, then buying a dress from someone other than Turner might not be as frightening an experience as she had thought.

In fact, just the prospect of ordering a dress

from a woman who, theoretically, would *like* to sell it rather than coaxing another out of Turner seemed exciting. Mattie's heart picked up its pace as she contemplated the possibility of buying more than one.

"But," William continued, "if I might make the suggestion, I should tell the dressmaker to make Pamela's in white. White is still generally considered most suitable for ingenues."

"Yes, thank you for that advice. I certainly shall." Mattie peered up at him and shyly asked, "But what about me? I suppose that for a woman of my age, appearing in white would seem quite foolish?"

"Foolish? No. But it would be a terrible waste when you would look so much more fetching in colors. For you—" William studied her, and as he looked, the lines of his face softened, making her pulse beat queerly "—either blue to match your eyes or a pale pink."

"Pink?" Mattie heard her voice squeak and cleared it. She didn't know why it had chosen to desert her just then, but she was not used to such close scrutiny.

"Yes." He smiled, and with a pang, she thought again how lucky Pamela would be if this man loved her. "You must have pink to match your roses."

This reference, as she supposed, to his Great Lie made her laugh, and her fluttering subsided. Then the others came in, and Mattie rose to let Pamela sit near William.

She listened with one ear to Gerald's excited account of the fox cubs they had discovered on their ride, and his and Pamela's plans for a hunt the next year, while she observed the other two as discreetly as she could. Her anxiety was mounting, for she had never yet seen any sign to suggest that William was in love with Pamela. He might be the most splendid catch for any girl, but she could not be happy unless he loved her daughter, too.

The gentlemen departed soon after this, William giving as his excuse the fact that Gerald smelled of the stable and should change out of his riding clothes, but Mattie wished he had appeared more reluctant to leave Pamela. Pamela, too, had not seemed to care for William's departure. She was spending so much time with Gerald in all her favorite pursuits that she scarcely knew William any better than she had when they'd first met.

Mattie tried not to let such worries disturb her. The date of her rout was approaching, and she could do nothing to stop it even though its original purpose no longer existed. She had hoped that it would show William that Pamela was too young to make him happy, but that was something she no longer desired.

If William came to that conclusion as a result of the rout or of anything else, then he would surely return to London and stop calling on them. Mattie knew that for her own sake, as well as her daughter's, that would not make her happy. Since they had met him, their whole lives had changed. No two days were ever alike. Each morning had the promise that something exciting might happen, and Mattie had discovered that she liked surprises.

What if William abandoned them and they were left once more to their own devices?

That very afternoon, as promised, a card was sent over from Norton Abbey giving the name and direction of Lady Westbury's modiste. Before she could forget to do so again, Mattie ordered up the carriage and took Pamela to call upon the woman directly.

She had planned to make an appointment only, and perhaps to see some of the dressmaker's patterns, but she and Pamela were warmly greeted at the door, and Madame Riviere, as the dressmaker was called, insisted she could see them at once.

Then Mattie had no time to be confused or flustered, for Madame Riviere took her firmly in hand. She saw that her customers were comfortably seated, supplied them with tea and biscuits, and brought out the books of patterns to choose from.

Mattie was so delighted with what she saw, and so surprised to see how the fashions had changed since she had last bothered to check, she knew that one dress apiece would not be near enough. Very firmly, she ordered six gowns for each—two morning gowns, one walking dress, and one new riding habit, as well as two that would be appropriate for evening—and gave instructions to have them delivered at intervals.

Money was no object, of course, but she did not want Turner's feelings to be hurt, and this way, with the deliveries coming a week or two apart, she would gradually become accustomed to the idea of being assisted with her work. Mattie made a note to herself to send Gilly down for some new dresses, too.

Mattie left Madame Riviere's with the feeling of someone who had just discovered the secrets of life. The sense of oppression under which she had suffered for some time whenever she'd thought of Pamela's London season had now lifted to the point that she could envision its prospect without terror. Every day that she had been learning how to cope outside her own self-imposed exile had brought its piece of a major revelation: that living in the world might not be so very bad.

A sense of excitement accompanied this. Mattie knew that she was looking forward to her rout, not with dread, but with a trembling anticipation, as nothing else in her life had yet inspired.

This was all brought to an end when Mrs. Puckeridge delivered her dreadful news.

That lady, unbeknownst to Mattie, had been suffering from a profound sense of injustice. On the duchess's behalf, she had called upon Mr. Jones, the caterer, only to be told—very politely to be sure, for no one would wish to offend the rector's wife—that Mr. Jones had already presented his services to Her Grace upon the request of Lord Westbury himself.

She had encountered a similar story from each tradesman in the village. Lord Westbury had sent down his card to each of the men she had planned to recommend with the request that they call upon the duchess with regard to her rout. He had stolen a march on her, and the fact that the gentleman in question knew nothing of his sins did not weigh with her in the least. It was she who was supposed to be the duchess's right-hand friend and confidante. Not his lordship.

The only comfort she could derive from finding herself useless to the impending event was to resort to a tactic she told herself that she abhorred. But she could not let Her Grace of Upavon be so shamefully used. His lordship was playing a devious game, and so the duchess should be told.

Mattie received Mrs. Puckeridge as warmly as she could, despite the fact that she could not quite like her. Mattie could see that the woman was operating under a sense of ill use, though she did not know why.

Consequently, she spent a great deal of time asking after Mrs. Puckeridge's children, and the rector, and the rectory, until she could see some relaxation in her visitor's carriage. An offering of tea, poured out with Mattie's own hands, did much to soften the other woman's demeanor as well.

It was not long before the talk turned to the rout, and Mrs. Puckeridge asked stiffly how Mattie's arrangements were progressing.

Mattie saw no reason to withhold the details, so she described the proposed party with all the enthusiasm she had begun to feel for it. Soon she realized that her happy chatter had brought a frown to Mrs. Puckeridge's face.

She faltered and asked, "Is anything the matter?"

Mrs. Puckeridge clasped her hands in her lap and pursed her lips. "I do not like to be the bearer of bad tidings, but I feel it to be my duty under the circumstances."

"Good heavens, what is it?" Mattie asked. "Has the caterer been taken ill?"

Mrs. Puckeridge scoffed. "Mr. Jones, taken ill? It is not very likely, is it, when it is his wife does all the work, and he merely does the speaking for her? No, Your Grace, I did not come here to speak of him."

"Who is it, then? One of the maids? Madame Riviere, the modiste?"

Mrs. Puckeridge straightened in her chair. "Have you ordered dresses from that woman?"

"Yes. Dear me. Is there some reason I should not have? But Will—his lordship did say that—"

"His lordship, is it? I should have known, not but what I should have supposed you would come to me to recommend a dresser, instead of asking a gentleman's opinion on the subject. And I would have offered first, but I understood as how you had a dresser of your own."

"I do," Mattie said, understanding at last the cause of her visitor's resentment. "And that is why I did not ask your advice at once, as grateful as I was over your help with the guest list, but you see, I—" She stopped before confessing her forgetfulness to Mrs. Puckeridge, who would only scorn it, Mattie was certain.

"Mrs. Puckeridge," she said, straightening her own shoulders, "if there is something you believe I should know, I wish you would tell it to me at once. This veiled sort of talk is making me very uneasy, I assure you."

"I do not like to be the bearer of bad tidings," that lady insisted upon repeating, "but I did not feel it right to keep silent when I knew you was being fooled."

"Being fooled?" Mattie felt a sudden sinking in the pit of her stomach. "By whom and about what? Be specific, if you please."

"By Lord Westbury himself!" Mrs. Puckeridge tucked her chin in a pose of self-righteousness. "Not but what it shames me to inform you. I would not think it of his lordship, if his mama had not told me of the scheme herself."

"Told you of what scheme?" Mattie's breath had nearly deserted her, but she managed to ask this much. William was fooling her? Please, Lord, no.

Mrs. Puckeridge bent forward to pat her hand. "There, there. I knew how it was as soon as I called at the Joneses and heard Lord Westbury had been around about the rout. What, I says to myself, would his lordship want with a caterer when he never stays more than two nights running in his own house? Then I thought of what her ladyship had been telling me, soon as she knew about the rout being planned."

Please stop this stalling, Mattie wanted to say, but she could not speak. She could only wait in as calm a manner as she could manage for the woman to go on.

Mrs. Puckeridge was smiling smugly now. She had got Mattie's attention, and seemed so satisfied with herself that Mattie knew a brief moment of hope. Perhaps the rector's wife was so full of mischief—or malice; Mattie hardly knew the difference—that she had taken pleasure in making a story up.

"It's this property," the woman finally said.

"Westbury Manor—you know its history, I am sure."

"I know something of it, of course." Pammy's dowry. How could I forget my suspicions about Pammy's dowry?

"Her ladyship says that it's his lordship's intention to woo Lady Pamela in order to get it back. You ought to hear her speak of it. She's quite proud, for it was her idea that put him up to it, as she admitted to me only two weeks ago. That day you came to me, in fact."

Mrs. Puckeridge continued, unaware that she was giving herself away, "I had just called on her ladyship, meaning to give her the good news about your rout, when she told me it was in honor of her son and Lady Pamela, no doubt, as a result of this match she had been scheming for. Then she gave me to understand what his lordship's interest was in the match."

Mattie felt like retching. She knew her daughter's heart had not been engaged, but still ... something inside her was breaking. "You say," she stammered, "Lord Westbury wants to marry my daughter for this property? And for no other reason?"

Mrs. Puckeridge answered reluctantly, "She did say as how his lordship was quite pleased with Lady Pamela. Called her charming and such like." Then she asked tentatively, "I hope no engagement has been arrived at. I would not like to have spoken if—"

"No," Mattie said firmly, though her lips were quivering. "There has been no agreement reached, and there will not be. You need have no qualms on that score."

Mrs. Puckeridge sat back with a smile on her face. And she would stay on, no matter how Mattie tried to discourage her with silence, until eventually even she could not fail to take the hint and took herself off.

Mattie sat alone for several minutes after her visitor had left, trying to compose her feelings. All their fun, all their delight together, had been nothing but a sham. She had been suspicious of William's interest from the start, and yet she had let herself be wooed and swayed by a cunning stranger. She had opened up, had taken risks she had never taken before. And she had almost cost her daughter her heart.

There would be nothing for it but to give the rout as planned. Too many people were counting on it, the tradesmen and the neighbors. But she would see to it that William could not pull off any more of his tricks.

Mattie was on the point of rising to go confess to Gilly how she had let herself be duped when the sound of an arrival at the front door burst upon her notice.

## Chapter Eight

"Uncle Cosmo!"

Mattie perceived her visitor, descending heavily from his carriage, and ran to throw herself upon his chest.

"There, there, puss." The present Duke of Upavon reddened and chuckled. "No need to knock me down."

Curbing her impulsive behavior—the result of her recent discovery, she knew—Mattie released her husband's brother and straightened his neckcloth, while gazing upon his welcome features.

Cosmo Staveley was immediately recognizable as a relative of Lady Pamela, his niece. He possessed the same curly blond hair, now reduced to a tonsure, the same rosy complexion easily turned to red, and the same tendency to girth, though Cosmo, under the influence of excellent food and drink, had long since converted that tendency into substance.

Mattie's unbridled welcome had put him to the blush, but he asked astutely, "What's the matter, puss? What's got you in such a fret?"

"Oh, we are all at sixes and sevens at the moment." Mattie regretted her carelessness already, and she was determined not to burden him with her troubles. "We're giving a rout, and I suppose all the fuss has put me into a dither."

"A rout?" Cosmo's face altered comically. He took on the pallor of a man whose last meal has suddenly revolted. "Not tonight, is it? Wouldn't have come if I'd known. Serves me right, you'll say, for arriving unannounced."

"I shall say no such thing," Mattie replied. "But no, it is not for today. It's on for tomorrow night."

Relief flooded his cheeks with pink. "That gives me time to make my escape on the morrow. Only came to see how you go on, you know."

"And that was dear of you, Cosmo. Why don't you come in, and we'll try to make you comfortable while you are here."

Mattie was grateful for his unexpected visit, which would keep her from thinking too much about William. At least, she hoped that it would. And, while seeing Cosmo settled into his old room and ordering up a dinner that was sure to please him, she was able for the moment to put her hurt aside.

However, between the time when Pamela went off to bed and the hour that Mattie and Cosmo settled down to their game of cards, she spent a half hour with Gilly in the drawing room waiting for Cosmo to finish his port, and all her heartache returned.

Cosmo had not seemed to notice, but as soon as Gilly excused herself for the evening, he raised his eyes from his cards and said, "Out with it, puss. There's something troubling you, and it don't take a genius to see."

"Oh . . ." Mattie waved a hand, trying to appear as if it were nothing. His perspicacity had taken her by surprise, and she wondered just how much her feelings showed. She had taken such pains to hide them from Gilly, a sudden reticence to confide having overtaken her when she might have shared them, but she had never expected Cosmo to be the one to ferret them out.

"No use trying to bam me." He reached across the table and gave her cheek a pinch. "Knew there was something wrong, soon as I saw all your bloom had gone missing. Not money, is it? Pamela playing the horses?" He shook his head and scolded her, "Only to come to me if it is."

"No, dearest. I am afraid it has nothing to do with money. You know how well His Grace provided for me, and if he had not, how could I ever forget your generosity?"

"Mine?" Cosmo's brows flew up. "What have I ever given you?"

Mattie smiled lovingly at him. "Have you forgotten how you insisted that I should take His Grace's servants to live with me?"

Cosmo blushed to the tips of his ears. "Nothing generous about it. Last thing a man wants is to be saddled with his brother's servants. Besides—" a rueful expression crossed his face "—always treated me like some interloper.

"But—" he caught himself up short "—out with it, now. What's toward?"

Mattie sighed and answered honestly, "It has something to do with our neighbor, Lord Westbury. He has been dangling after Pammy, and I've only now discovered—"

She broke off, somehow unwilling to state the case as badly as she had been forced to see it.

"Discovered what? Fellow's not a loose screw, is he? Seems to me, I've never heard anything bad about him."

"Not a loose screw, no." She paused. "At least, I do not think so." Mattie stared at the hands clenched in her lap. "I'm afraid that his motives for pursuing Pamela—although perhaps quite acceptable by society's standards—do not entirely meet with mine. I want something better for her, that is all."

"Want me to send the fellow about his business? Could, you know. Head of the family and all that." Cosmo's round, pink face was screwed up with anxiety.

Gratitude warmed Mattie's heart. "I know you could, dearest. But I think I should be the one to do it, as Pamela's only remaining parent."

"Could marry me, you know." Cosmo squirmed in his chair. "Very fond of you and all that. Certain you would make me very happy."

Mattie's eyes flooded with tears, and her lips quivered inexplicably. "No, thank you, dearest. You mustn't feel the need to do that."

Cosmo's expression changed into a strange combination of worry and guilt. "Aren't bothered by what parson'll say, are you? Brother's wife and all that. Superstitious mumbo jumbo."

Mattie gave a watery chuckle. She left her chair and went around to hug him. "No, dearest. It is just that you are perfectly comfortable as you are, and you don't need me to disturb you."

She planted a kiss on the top of his bald pate, and Cosmo turned the shade of a ripe cherry.

"Wouldn't bother me," he said, looking down at

the table. "Never bothered m'brother. Said you were a good girl and I should look after you."

"And you have." Mattie rested her cheek sadly on his head. She did not know why his proposal had distressed her so much, but in spite of her affection for him, which was very real, for a moment she had felt a moment of fear—some eerie sense of history being repeated.

"You've come to see how we go on, and I do feel better for having you here, however briefly. You must check on us as often as you like."

She left his side to retake her seat, and Cosmo confided sheepishly, "On my way back from New-market, you know. Right on the way. No trouble at all."

"I am very glad to hear it. Now, let us forget my foolish worries and play, shall we?"

Mattie took up her hand, and for the rest of the evening, was able to entertain her guest without too much effort to appear restored. It helped that many years ago, she had learned to ignore her own desires for the sake of others.

What she wanted now was not terribly clear, but she knew that she had no wish to face William tomorrow.

The next day passed in a rush of preparations and last-minute changes. Cosmo insisted upon parting after breakfast so as not to be in the way, although Mattie supposed he was really terrified by the possibility that his carriage might break down and cause him to stay and face her guests.

When he bid her good-bye at the door, he paused to say, "Don't let yourself fret too much, puss. Come to see me in Bath any time you want. Only have to speak . . . and so on."

Mattie thanked him with a tight hug that turned his words into stammers and sent him on his way.

By that evening, Mattie was all atremble. The rooms were decorated to her satisfaction, her new dress delivered in time, the food and games all taken care of, and Gilly set to play accompaniment if anyone cared to dance. But Mattie knew that William would be there, and she did not know how to meet his gaze without revealing her bitter disappointment.

His flowers had arrived after noon. One box for her and one for Pamela. Mattie watched her daughter open the card that had been addressed to her and turn pink with pleasure as she read the message. Mattie did not ask to see it, nor could she bring herself to open the small white note that accompanied her posy of pale pink roses and feathery Queen Anne's lace.

She debated whether or not to wear the flowers. They were so beautiful. It pained her to turn her back on them, and in the end, she decided to wear them. She did not want to speak to William at the rout and suspected that he might question her about the flowers' arrival if he did not see them on her breast.

The guests arrived mostly in pairs of mother and daughter or mother and son, though some came in larger family groups. The boys bowed nervously; the girls made awkward curtsies; a few giggled noisily depending upon their gender and the strictness of either parent.

But no matter how anxious they were when they entered the door, the same humor pervaded the lot of them: high spirits in youthful bodies, and an expectation of having a good time.

Mattie found that Gilly had been correct. It was not long before the young people found each other and launched themselves into happy chatter. Their parents did as well, lounging about the perimeter of the room in chairs that had been provided while keeping eyes on their charges. Mattie's own duties soon devolved into making certain that none of their guests dropped back shyly or succeeded in feeling left out.

Pamela mingled with the guests as best she could, though Mattie observed sadly that her daughter did not shine in company any better than she had herself. Pammy's manners were a shade abrupt perhaps; when something surprised her, her skin flushed as readily as her father's and Cosmo's. Mattie could only hope that her daughter would make a new friend or two from among the group.

The arrival of William and Gerald appeared to cheer Pamela, and it was not long before Gerald and she had put their heads together. From that moment on, Mattie felt few worries on Pamela's score. Gerald, as one of the oldest and liveliest boys present, an acknowledged leader among them in sports, managed to engage the others in a spirited round of games.

Mattie had greeted William no differently from any other guest and quickly turned her back on him to speak to someone else. He had not tried to dominate her time, but instead chatted in a neighborly fashion with her guests. She tried not to think of him at all, but she could not keep her gaze from wandering to him. She noticed how effortlessly he could fall into conversation with persons he scarcely knew.

She could see, too, how pleased her guests were to receive his attention. He was accomplished at putting people at their ease—as he had her, she reminded herself. A stab of pain so intense she could hardly bear it made her turn away from him again.

At the stroke of ten, when the party was winding down, someone was heard to mention how diverting it would be to dance. It was never clear where the suggestion had come from, but it was soon taken up by all the young people. Mattie gave the order for the tables and chairs to be swept aside to make a dance floor.

Gilly took her place at the pianoforte. Some couples formed quite readily, and Mattie was relieved to see that Gerald, instead of his brother, led Pamela out. She had not yet had time to warn Pamela about William's false attentions, though with a heavy heart she supposed she must soon do so.

She went about the room to see if any others would venture to dance if she could find them a partner.

This job was no sooner completed than William appeared at her elbow. Mattie could feel his presence long before she saw him. The heat from his body set her cheeks aflame, though she tried as hard as she could to ignore him.

"Mattie."

He claimed her attention as she had known he

would. It would take more than a little ignoring to dissuade a Norton.

"Would you honor me with this dance?"

His request robbed her of composure. A fluttering began in the pit of her stomach and spread through her, making her both angry and flustered at once.

"But I cannot dance! It wouldn't be at all appropriate."

"I cannot think why not. I believe you promised me one."

"I—" It was true, she remembered, he had spouted some nonsense about reserving him a dance, but she had thought that was only part of his teasing. The trouble with William was, one never did know exactly what he was thinking.

"I did not mean it," Mattie said painfully. "I do not intend to dance. I have my guests to think of."

She ventured a look at his face and saw that he was frowning in a way she had never seen before. Was there anger in his eyes? Hurt? *Surely not!* But there was something that weakened her resolve.

"Mattie, is something the matter? You are not acting your usual self. Has someone said something to upset you?"

She attempted a laugh. "Lord Westbury, I am afraid you are reading more into my manner than there is. I am quite busy, you know. Hosting."

A hint of a smile lit his eyes, but his brows were still lowered as he searched her face. "And doing a fine job of it, too. One would think you had entertained all your life. Your party is a roaring success, Mattie."

It would not have been if it weren't for you, Mattie wanted to say. But the thought made her sad. William knew just what help she needed and how and when to supply it, but she would never have his help again. The price she had paid in broken trust could not be worth the gain.

Her expression must have betrayed her thoughts, for he said quickly, "I know there is something. You've been ignoring me all evening, and I know when you are unhappy."

"I—" Mattie found her chin was quivering. "I cannot discuss this now. Not with guests here. But if you care to call again—in another week or so, perhaps—"

"Another week? I think we should discuss it now." With a tightening of his jaw, he turned her and started steering her toward the door to the saloon.

Mattie tried to protest that she must not leave her guests, but he guided her firmly, saying, "Your guests are all happy. We will not be a moment," and managed to usher her through the crowded room without giving the appearance that anything was wrong.

The company all parted for him, bowing amicably, and he returned their notice sufficiently so that none appeared to suspect that he was pushing her out of the room. Mattie cast a glance behind her and saw that everything was, in fact, under control. The first dance had come to a halt, and the children were mingling with little restraint. Gilly had found another piece of music and was already picking out the first keys by the time she and William reached the door.

He showed her through it, down the corridor, and into her morning room, which was deserted, then closed the door behind them. Mattie's heart was beating loudly in her ears, so that she barely heard his questions as he turned her to face him.

"What is it, Mattie? What has happened? Have I done anything to offend you?"

Yes, she wanted to say. He had done something to wound her deeply, but to say so would not really be fair. He had never been anything in her presence but polite and considerate. It was not really William's fault, perhaps, that society was so mercenary, it had led him to court her daughter for all the wrong reasons.

"No, of course not." Mattie spoke with a breathless hitch in her throat. Her knees were shaking. "But perhaps it is as well that we have this talk. I have come to a decision that may—a—a decision regarding your visits to this house."

His brow descended then, in a heavy black line that might have frightened her if his tone had not been so gentle. "And what is that decision, pray?"

"I—have decided—I am afraid I must ask you not to call again."

"Why?"

How like William, she thought, not to accept what she said.

"You must not dangle after Pamela any longer." She was on firm ground now. She could be strong for Pammy.

"Dangle?"

"Yes."

"After Pamela?"

"No—I mean, yes—" Mattie girded herself for his next question, which was sure again to be *why*. "You must not do it."

"You silly goose!"

He released her elbow, which she had hardly been aware of his holding, she had been so unnerved. With a sharp, sudden laugh, he ran one hand through his hair.

"What do you mean?" she asked. She had not expected his reaction to be amusement.

But when he raised his face to speak to her, she saw that amusement was only one of his emotions. Frustration, confusion, and a touch of anger lurked in his eyes as well.

"Mattie, what made you think I was dangling after Pamela?"

"But aren't you?"

"No, you foolish darling. I'm 'dangling,' as you put it, after you. *You're* the one I want."

"Oh, dear." Mattie felt as if the air had been knocked from her lungs. She had already been having trouble breathing, for she did not like scenes. She had managed to avoid them all her life, but she could not avoid this one, and the anticipation of it had robbed her of breath.

And now this . . .

She peered at William, and saw that behind his amused look was another one, quite serious.

The strength went out of her knees. She fell onto the chair behind her. "Oh, dear . . . What a bumblebroth!"

"Is it so bad?" William dropped to one knee in front of her. This position brought his handsome face closer than it had ever been to hers before, and in spite of his question, she saw that he was laughing at her response.

But this could not be happening, Mattie told herself. He must be confused. And there was a reason for his confusion, if she could only ignore his proximity long enough to think of what it was.

"You can't want me," she said, remembering the problem in a sudden burst of lucidity. "The property belongs to Pamela."

"Which property?"

"The one you want." She did not know why he was looking so puzzled. If anyone knew what he wanted, it should be William. "Westbury Manor. This house. It belongs to Pamela, not to me."

Understanding swept his features, followed by a tightly controlled anger. For one moment, Mattie felt a flash of guilt-filled regret that the house was not hers.

"I do not care one whit about Westbury Manor. But I can see that someone has told you that I do, and I would like to know who that someone was."

Mattie felt a rush of some emotion warming her cheeks. Mortification—mixed with—mixed with hope? "I—yes, someone did mention to me that you wanted to recover the property, but I—I could not really tell you who—I—"

William nodded, his jaw clenched with restraint. "Very well. You do not have to tell me. That is not what matters most, although I can guess that either my mother or some crony of hers was responsible. The important thing is that I am in love with you."

"But—you can't be!" What would Gilly have to say? William could not love her. He was younger than she was.

"Why?" There he was again with his *whys*. "You are quite lovable, you know."

"But—" Mattie knew she must put an end to this declaration. He had taken her hand in his strong, masculine one, and the strangest things were happening to her palm. A tingling had invaded it, as if her hand had been frozen and now was thawing. . . .

"I am older than you," she managed to choke out, even though her speech was hampered by a shortness of breath. She must be firmer. "You are nothing but a boy."

A glint lit his eyes. "It has been many years since a woman's called me that."

What woman? How many women? Ridiculous questions flittered through her brain, but she pushed them aside. "You must feel the difference in our ages," she protested feebly.

"Would you like to know what I feel?"

Before she knew it, William's face had moved closer. She focused on his eyes, such deep dark pools of mystery. His nearness had her frozen in place. He seemed so purposeful. So sure.

Mattie closed her eyes just as he touched his lips to hers. She could breathe his aroma, the same scent that filled her nostrils with sweet tobacco, leather, and soap. His lips moved softly against hers, like some luxurious cloud urging her to float, drawing her upward out of herself. A languid heat stole through her body, a warmth more deeply satisfying than a sip of brandy on a cold winter day. . . .

It was a second or more before she realized that William had pulled away. Her lips were still puckered, her eyes still closed dreamily, when he asked in a far-off voice, "Do you still think I am too young?"

Mattie's eyes flew open to find William regarding her with laughter in his gaze. His tender look, a hint of deeper desire, caused her heart to flutter.

"I—I don't know. This is quite sudden—you see, I thought you wanted—"

"You thought I wanted Pamela. Yes, and that was quite silly of you, if you stop to think how much time I've been spending with you."

A blush and a smile ran together on her cheeks. "I—perhaps so—but still—"

A consciousness of where they were suddenly burst in upon her. "Good Lord! I've forgotten my guests!"

"Yes, you have. I think that is a good sign," William teased. Then his face grew serious. "Mattie, I did not mean to spring this upon you. If it weren't for these gossips, I would have taken more time. Not that I needed it, but perhaps you might."

"I must get back to my guests," Mattie said, suddenly agitated on their behalf. She had been dreadfully remiss. What would everyone think of her?

"Yes, and I will let you get back to them in just a second. But please, think about what I have said. Think about how you feel. May I come to the garden tomorrow for your answer?"

"Yes—tomorrow." She was still unsure how to answer him, but a night's reflection ought to bring some counsel. For the moment, she could only drift in a sea of amazement. Her lips were still tingling. Her heart was beating like a bird in rapid flight.

Then Mattie realized she did not even know what William's question had been, but she was too stunned to consider, too flustered to think. All she knew for certain was that she could not ignore her company any longer.

William helped her to rise. He refrained from taking her into his arms, but he did lift her hand to his lips.

"Don't worry," he said. "I only want to make you happy, Mattie. I love you."

He drew her to the door and let her precede him from the room. Her limbs felt heavy and light at the same time, like floating lead. Mattie had never felt so strange before, so divinely tingling yet limp as a sleepy kitten all at the same time.

Somehow she managed to get through the rest of the evening. The party soon broke up; the parents were anxious not to overstay their welcome despite their children's pleas for one more dance. Mattie saw each person to the door, and only hoped later that she had remembered to thank them for coming.

She was not sure what she had said to them. The only parting that stood out in her memory was William's as he pulled Gerald from the group. If she had been one of the guests, she would not have noticed anything different about him. His manners were so perfect, he might have been taking his leave of any hostess rather than one to whom he had just made a declaration of love.

This was true until he actually stood facing her, and only then, if someone had been standing by her side, would he have seen a difference, the slight softening of William's etched features, a lingering gaze that managed to convey a promise for tomorrow, a hand clasped perhaps a little longer than was customary. If it were not for these signs, Mattie might have thought that she'd dreamed the scene in her morning room.

Later that night, as she lay awake in bed, she did imagine it again: William's kiss—no kiss of a boy, that, or so she supposed. He had said that he loved her. He'd said that he wanted her.

Mattie had never felt wanted before.

She thought back to her marriage to His Grace. She remembered his proposal, if one could call it that. She had been sixteen, slightly more than Pamela's age, when he had called her into his library and asked her to sit down.

His Grace often requested her company after dinner when he needed a partner for cards, but this time the card table had not been set out.

"Everything well, Mattie? Are you happy here, girl?"

"Yes."

"Nothing you find lacking? Nothing you want particularly?"

"No, I think I have everything I need."

"Good girl! That's what I like about you, Mattie. None of the foolishness these other girls get up to! I daresay you don't even know what

I'm talking about, but you may take it from me that it is all foolishness!"

Mattie remembered wondering then what sort of foolishness other girls got up to, and asking herself if she might not like it. She had been feeling lonely for more than a year, and she sometimes wished she had other children her age to play with. Miss Fotheringill had told her stories about London and society and all the balls she would no doubt attend when His Grace brought her out, and Mattie had begun to look forward to them.

But His Grace had gone on, "Well, since you seem happy enough, I thought I would give you a nice surprise."

Her ears pricked up. She thought that perhaps he meant to take her on a trip as he sometimes did to visit one of his friends, or maybe he'd ordered a special plant as a gift for her. His Grace gave her presents from time to time when the mood suited him or he thought she might be pining for something new.

"How'd you like to be a duchess, heh?"

His question did come as a surprise, that was certain. Mattie did not know if she would like to be a duchess; it was not something she had ever given any thought to.

"You mean, be like you," she asked, "only I'd still be me?" It was an incoherent reply, but it seemed to please His Grace.

"That's the thing precisely. Mattie, you're as sharp as a tack. One reason I like you, see. You can marry me and be a duchess." His Grace rubbed his woolly blond head and turned a deeper shade of pink. "Need an heir, see. Duty to the family and all that. Never much in the petti-coat line, as you know, but with you at the reins, Mattie, I ought to come up a winner." He chuck-led and mumbled something that made no sense to her, "Nothing to it, they say."

"Do you want me to marry you?" Mattie re-membered asking. Even as accustomed as she was to His Grace's way of speaking, Mattie was not certain she had understood him this time. Marriage was beyond her horizon. She had only dimly begun to think of what it might entail, knowing only that the point of all those balls she would soon attend would be to find her a hus-band.

"Don't necessarily want you to," His Grace an-swered honestly. "Need a wife. Thought of you. Good girl and all that. Thought you might like to be a duchess, since they say every girl and her nursemaid wants to be one."

"Thank you," Mattie said, for she saw that he meant it kindly, although the nebulous dreams she'd been having would now have to be put aside. She did not particularly want to marry His Grace, but she could see that he meant to give her a treat in spite of his own reticence to marry, and she did not want to hurt his feelings.

He had always been good to her, ever since the day many years ago when her parents had died and she had been sent to live with him. He had patted her nervously on the head, told her to be a good girl, and stated that he was sure they would go along famously.

"That's settled, then," he had finished on this new occasion. "We'll be married in a trice. Then we can go on as we have without too much folde-rol."

He'd dismissed her with a pinch on the cheek. "Nothing to worry about," he'd said. "I'm sure we'll go along like two peas in a pod."

"Yes, His Grace."

He'd chuckled. "Better get that right, m'girl, or we'll have the wags down on us. It's *Your* Grace when you're speaking to me, you know."

"Very well, Your Grace."

Mattie remembered returning to her room and seeing the color of Gilly's face when she heard the news. Gilly had turned white as a lily, and her voice had trembled when she'd asked, "Do you say you have already accepted him?"

"Yes."

"My dearest child—if I'd only known!"

Then Gilly had said nothing more, not then, not ever, until her recent admission that she should have protested to His Grace.

Mattie thought about her subsequent life, when the secrets of marriage had been revealed to her. She could not say that she'd enjoyed that aspect of marriage, but neither had His Grace.

He had tried to conceive an heir, once, and then semiannually, until Pamela had finally been born. When she had turned out to be a girl, he had patted Mattie on the shoulder sadly and said, "Looks like this heir business is more diffi-cult than I thought. By Jupiter! It is too hard! Better leave it to the younger fellows. Cosmo says he don't want to be a duke, but he can jolly well take my place."

Then he'd examined Pamela and a flicker of interest had lit his face. "Taking little thing, ain't she? Wonder if she'll cry much."

"I don't really know," Mattie had said, eyeing her bundle with a jumble of feelings. She was sorry she had not given His Grace an heir since he had seemed to want one, but he did not appear to be severely disappointed. And from her perspective, the baby in the cradle had been as beautiful a being as she had ever seen.

No, she could reflect with tears tonight, she could never truly be sorry she had married His Grace, not when he had given her Pamela. She had never been sorry, not even when they had gone to London and she'd been given a glimpse of what she'd missed: the handsome young men; the rounds of parties and schemes. She had missed them all, but His Grace had given her a safe place to live, where none of the gossips who'd said she had married him for his position could possibly ever harm her.

And now came William, seeking her out in spite of her retirement. He said that he loved her. He wanted her, and she thought she knew what he meant by the fire in his eyes and the corresponding warmth that built inside her.

During her short tenure in London, Mattie had heard other whispers, about men and their mistresses. She had seen the glances some men had given to women, when their spouses were not watching.

Could she dare to be William's mistress? She did not know how he planned to manage the affaire, but she knew that she could trust William to find a way. If he wanted to be with her, he would find the time and place to do so in secrecy.

And would she?

Mattie felt the heat from his kiss burning into her thoughts, and she knew that she would take the dare. She knew that she loved William, and the lure of his embraces would be too strong to pass up. This would be her first chance—and surely her last—to have a love. She would give herself to William, her true self that she had buried away long ago for the convenience of a dear old man.

Tears filled her eyes as she remembered His Grace's last words to her. "You're a good girl, Mattie. A good girl to put up with an old man. Don't fret for me, mind."

His Grace would not have understood Mattie's need to have William, even for the space of a brief affaire, but neither would he begrudge her the try.

# Chapter Nine

*T*he next morning, Mattie trembled with anticipation as she made her way into the garden to meet William.

Her roses were in bloom. Moss, cabbage, and sweetbrier, pale pink and pearly white, lay open to the sun like velvety offerings to Venus. On the tops of the walls, birds flitted between the glossy vines, playing their own flirting games. It seemed to Mattie that her garden shared her sense of expectancy, filled as it was with the sharp smell of fertile earth, the soft whispering of leaves, and the humming of bees as they sipped upon nectar.

But William was not there yet.

Seeing this, Mattie felt a twinge of nervous disappointment, but she consoled herself with the thought that he would be along shortly. The problem was that she was not quite sure what to do with herself. She could not very well work without soiling the pinafore Turner had sewn. Mattie had worn it so as not to arouse the servants' suspicions.

Convinced that mud would not be conducive to romance, Mattie resolved to wait in demure idleness. She stood with an eye discreetly turned toward the stables, by which direction William was sure to come.

She waited, fidgeting, for several minutes. It proved a vastly uncomfortable thing to do since the poses she affected as being most likely to show her in her best light could not be held indefinitely. Her neck became stiff from holding her chin at an arrested angle, and her back grew sore from being stiff. She started at the snap of every twig and the rustle of every blade of grass until she thought her head might fly off at the next sound. Disappointment built inside her, and the deeply disquieting feeling that she might have imagined the whole had begun to take hold of her when William's deep voice came from behind her.

"Mattie."

She spun and jumped backward. Her pulse began a rapid beat, and she breathed, "Oh . . . It is you."

"Did I startle you?" Amusement lit William's eyes as he took a step closer.

"Oh, no . . . Well, yes. You see, I—" Staring at William, Mattie realized that she was seeing him in a new light, as her potential lover. His strong masculinity seeped through her defenses. His vigor echoed in her bones. A blush crept up her neck as he slowly walked toward her, and a rush of heat such as she'd never known made her stammer huskily, "I thought you might come around from the stables."

"I couldn't sleep," William said, taking her hands. His earnest gaze filled her with fear and joy. "I decided to walk instead." He searched her face. "I must know now, Mattie. Have you decided to accept me?"

"Yes." Her voice trembled on the response. "If you are sure you want me."

"Ah, Mattie." William swept her into his arms, and his voice sounded low near her ear. A delicious sense of strength surrounded her. "I think I have wanted you since that first day I saw you."

"Have you?" Joy bubbled up inside her. William kissed her, and her frightful quivering was replaced by a deeper yearning, an insistent hunger to move even closer to him.

"Tell me, Mattie," William insisted, his hands moving from her waist to her hips in a way that made her feel dizzy. "Do you love me? Tell me that you love me."

The absurdity of his question brought a smile to her lips. "Yes, of course I do. Else I should not be kissing you in this shameless way—" A sudden realization of what they were doing—and where—made her squeak, "William, you must let me go! What if the servants see us?"

"Let them." He ran kisses down her neck, and the sensation was so novel and so delicious that, at first, Mattie could not bring herself to stop him. She felt a strange and overwhelming desire for William to bury his lips between her breasts.

Then a sense of her own vulnerability, the knowledge that they must conduct their affaire discreetly or risk shattering her peace, gave her strength.

Gently, and breathlessly, she extricated herself from his grasp. With a reluctant grin, William accepted the distance she put between them, but kept hold of her hands.

Now that she could feel his dark, seductive gaze, shyness overcame Mattie again. She was not sure what they ought to say next. Should they discuss when and where they could meet?

William must have perceived her discomfort, for he dropped one of her hands and drew the other into the crook of his arm. "We could stroll in the garden if you like. Would that better suit your sense of propriety?"

"Yes, you must know that it would."

They walked, not looking at each other until both their pulses had steadied a bit. William led her toward a tall row of shrubbery. He seemed to be taking his time about discussing the arrangements that would have to be made—a discussion that would surely put her to the blush.

Of a sudden, he drew her behind the hedge and back into his arms. "There. Now we may be comfortable."

"William!" Mattie shrieked in a whisper. "What are you doing?"

"I'm making passionate love to you. Don't you like it?"

"I—I don't know. I think I like it excessively, but—I hardly know what to expect!"

"Don't know what to expect?" William held her away from him and searched her face. Whatever he saw there made his jaw tighten. "Mattie, I do not know what your marriage was like, but I aim to make love to you, and often. Does that disturb you?"

Mattie bit her lip to keep its quivering from betraying her. "I did not mean that entirely," she said painfully, "but you must know that His Grace was not—a young man—"

William gathered her gently into his arms. "You needn't say more. I will never hurt you, Mattie, but I desperately want to make love to you."

"Yes, I know."

"Answer me, then. Does the prospect frighten you?"

Mattie felt his arms go tense.

She examined her feelings—the excited hammering of her heart, the delicious weakness in her knees—then hid her face in his coat. "No."

"Thank God."

She heard his rush of relief, and the thought that she had pleased him gave her a burst of happiness.

"Have I rushed you, Mattie?" he asked. "It could not be soon enough for me, but I had planned to take longer. I had a feeling that you would need more time to feel as deeply for me as I do for you. If you wish, I will court you more slowly."

William's thoughtfulness brought tears into her eyes in the same moment that an unaccustomed greediness prompted her to say, "Yes, please. I would like that."

Gently he held her away, then planted a kiss upon her nose. "Perhaps I should send you roses?"

Mattie chuckled. "No, you needn't do that. I think I have enough of them."

"Then what would please you, my love? You have only to say."

A pulse started up in her throat as she asked, "I would like—very much—for you to tell me why you love me."

"Why." William considered. "Now, let me see. . . ."

Mattie giggled at his earnest expression.

"I simply could say that I do not know why. I cannot help myself. But I doubt that that would satisfy you."

Mattie shook her head, suppressing a dimple.

"Perhaps I could tell you the things I love about you? Would that do?"

"Yes," she said, trying to hide her eagerness. "That would be simple."

William's arms tightened about her waist. His lips softened as she gazed deeply into his dark eyes.

"I love the way you dress in faded old gowns," he said softly. "I love it that smudges find their way onto your nose. I love the way you seem blind to any mistakes your daughter makes, but that you blush for your own quite charmingly. I love it that—"

"But those are all faults!" Mattie protested, not sure that she wanted to hear more.

"Oh, no, my love. You are very wrong. Each of those things is a sign of your unspoiled nature and your generous heart. Those are what I love you for, Mattie."

When she peered up at him, still not convinced, he grinned. "I might want you because you are beautiful and have a splendid figure, but I love you because you are a kind and gentle soul, Mattie. There is no one else like you."

A catch filled her throat as she said, "I love you, too, William." She threw her arms shamelessly about his neck, and he held her tightly.

"There is one thing I would request," he murmured into her ear.

"What is that?" Mattie would do anything. She had never been so happy. At this point, she only wanted to know how they would manage to be together, for she did not think the shrubbery would be a comfortable place to meet.

"Promise me," William continued in a sober tone, "that once we are wed, you will go back to gardening in your outmoded gowns. They have the most glorious effect on my—"

"Married!" Mattie gasped as his words sank in. She pushed away in order to see him. "But we are not to be married!"

"Not ..." He frowned, and bewilderment clouded his features. "What the devil do you mean? I thought you said yes."

"I did. But not to marriage!"

Mattie waited for the truth to register on his face. When it did, she felt a stab of shame.

"Mattie, you cannot mean—you did not think that I was offering you *carte blanche*?"

The hint of anger in his voice made her wince. "But of course I thought so! What else could I think? You could not possibly mean to marry a woman of my age."

"I could mean it, and I do mean it. I have no intention of giving you a slip on the shoulder. You must think I'm the devil of a fellow."

"No, oh no." Mattie could see that he was hurt, but she would not blame herself. "You said nothing of marriage. How was I to know?"

"How? Did you think that I would so mistreat you? Haven't I just said how much I love you, Mattie?"

"Yes, but—" Distress clogged her throat. "Now, this *is* a bumblebroth!"

"It doesn't have to be one. Now that we are both clear on what I do want, you have only to say yes again."

"But I cannot!"

"For God's sake, why?" William ran one hand through his perfect locks.

Mattie stared at him helplessly, unable to believe that he would not understand. "The talk—the things people will say—"

"What things?"

"They will say that I robbed the cradle!"

"Nonsense. They will look at me with envy and say how clever I was to win you before the ton laid eyes upon you."

"No, William." Mattie's eyes filled with tears. "You cannot know—you cannot imagine the cruelty—"

He took her by the elbows and gave her a little shake. "What cruelty? What did they do to you, Mattie?"

She hung her head. She wanted to throw herself in William's arms, but she dared not. She had to make him see that it was impossible. "When I was first married, His Grace took me to London to be presented. Everyone turned their noses up at me. I heard what they said—they did not try to hide it. They said I had married him for his money and his position, but—" she grasped William by his lapels "—I did not, William! I had a fortune of my own."

William's lips curved indulgently, as if he failed to see how miserable she had been. "I know you did not," he said. "I think I know how it was. But that is all in the past, Mattie. It has nothing to do with us."

"Yes it does. Don't you see? They will remember that old scandal and say that I married just as callously the second time as I did the first."

"You're a grown woman now. You must not care for what people say."

"Not even Lady Westbury?"

"Particularly not my mother."

Mattie shook her head vehemently. "I cannot face her, William. Not her, not anyone. I cannot live through another scandal when I have Pamela to think of. You want a wife who can take her place in the ton, but I cannot be that person. They will say you should have chosen a wife who can give you children, that it was selfish of me to marry such an eligible man. I know how they think!"

William was smiling broadly now, as if she were simply being foolish. "You are taking a pet for nothing. Those people are not worth worrying about. And whether we have a child or not does not concern me overmuch. I mean to enjoy trying, but if we are unsuccessful, Gerald will make a fine viscount."

"But what about Gilly!" Mattie changed the subject, unwilling to talk about such issues as children, when she knew she would never have the chance to know William's child. "Miss Fotheringill, that is. I could not face her, William, and if I could not face Gilly, who loves me, how could I stand up in public with you?"

William's look became stern. "You refine too much upon your servants' feelings. I've noticed that you let them bully you. You must not let anyone bully you, Mattie!"

His tone, when he said this, was so overbearing that Mattie could only stare at him wryly.

A look of sheepishness came over his face, and he apologized, "There I go, doing it, too. I am sorry, Mattie. I will promise never to bully you again if you will marry me."

"But don't you see? Everyone does. I cannot stand up to people, William, and you must believe me. That is why I live the way I do. And I was happy enough. And then you came along, and I thought I could be perfectly happy to love you in private where no one would see or know—"

Mattie broke off at the disapproving look on his face. She gathered her courage and said, "I can be your mistress, William. I very much want to be your mistress. But I cannot be your wife."

"No, Mattie. I will have no backstairs affaire with you. You must marry me."

A determined gleam showed in his eyes as he took a step backwards. "I shall have to convince you. That is all."

Mattie held her quivering chin in the air. "You cannot."

"We shall see." A hint of sympathy tinged his gaze. "I sincerely hope that you are wrong."

"Oh, William—" Mattie reached to brush his cheek "—I do love you, but it would be too great a mistake. You must not try to persuade me."

"I am sorry to distress you, dearest, but I must."

Mattie could not speak. Her tears were too near the surface. She made a sign for him to go.

William raised her hand and kissed it before saying, "I shall call upon you soon. Don't worry yourself too much over this, Mattie. All will come right in the end. You will see."

Mattie wished she could believe him. As he turned to leave her, and crossed the great lawn on his way back home, she felt her heart would break. Her one great chance for happiness had come and gone. But she could not give in. She could not, either for Pamela's sake or for William's own.

If she married him, he would regret it as soon as the scandal erupted. He was not like His Grace. William moved about the world. He would not be happy with a wife whom society rejected.

Mattie turned and fled back into the house, the fabric of her peace all torn to shreds.

William walked rapidly, and by the time he reached his door, the greater part of his frustration had been worked off. He told himself that Mattie's reaction was precisely what he had feared it would be when he had determined to woo such a sensitive creature. He had long suspected that something had made her fearful of society, and it was for that reason he had decided to court her slowly.

Now that she had confirmed his intuition, he could imagine how it had happened. Mattie had wed her aged guardian, not out of passion, but out of innocence. At a sensitive age, she had been taken to London, only to discover that society frowned upon such a marriage. William could guess what assumptions had been made about a wealthy old bachelor and a beautiful young wife. Hadn't his mother insinuated much the same?

William's suspicion that Lady Westbury or one of her friends had tipped his hand before he was ready to declare himself made him clench his jaw now. But he would not waste time in anger. What was done was done, and whatever Mattie's fears were, he would soon overcome them. She had admitted that she loved him. With a burgeoning sense of joy, he acknowledged that the battle was half-won.

Arriving home, William was not particularly pleased to find his mother waiting for him. She accosted him in the hall before he could make for the relative sanctuary of his library, and said in an injured tone that she would be grateful for a few moments of his time.

William bowed to her and, restraining his impatience, waited for her to pass into the room before him.

"You wished to see me?" he asked, as he held a chair for her.

"I did," Lady Westbury announced. She seated herself with her shoulders back and her hands clasped firmly on her lap. "I mean to discover what you have been getting up to, William. I could not help noticing that you left the house this morning and set out on foot in the direction of Westbury Manor."

When William said nothing in response, but, instead, took his chair across from her and waited, she continued, "Your attentions in that quarter have been most pronounced, and I had allowed myself to be pleased. You have not always been wont to take my advice, but I had flattered myself that at least this once you had. Then I spoke to Gerald and discovered that he had made an appointment to ride with Lady Pamela this morning, just—or so he says—as he has done every morning this week."

Lady Westbury leaned forward. "Where have you been, pray, William, when your brother has been cavorting about the countryside with your intended bride and without you in attendance?"

William controlled the retort that sprang to his tongue. It took a few moments before the unmistakable humor of the situation restored his equanimity.

"I have been calling upon the duchess," he said politely, "and since she has been with me the greater part of each morning, I fail to see how she could be cavorting with Gerald."

His mother's nostrils flared. Her eyes widened as she braced herself to argue. "Whatever do you mean? I had supposed that we were discussing Lady Pamela. You will oblige me, William, by not speaking in riddles."

"I have spoken quite plainly, Mama. You, unfortunately, appear to be laboring under a misapprehension."

"Nonsense!" Lady Westbury fixed him with a stern eye. "I understand the circumstances quite clearly. You have made it your business—and in general I approve of such thoroughness—to be attentive to the girl's mother. But I would not abuse such a tactic, William. I am sure you have proven your worthiness to the duchess. It is time to focus on her daughter instead. I presume Lady Pamela will have some say in the matter."

"Do you think so?" William raised his eyebrows. "I am afraid that your notions of filial rights are far more liberal than my own."

Lady Westbury did not look pleased by this compliment. "If you mean to tease me, William, you will catch cold at it. I was not born yesterday, and I recognize your tone. You undoubtedly refer to my notions of propriety and mean to imply that you do not approve of such antiquated views. But let me tell you that an arranged marriage has far more chance of success than these runaway love matches one is forever reading about. I know Lady Pamela will see the wisdom in marrying whomever her mother has chosen for her."

"Will she? I wonder. . . ." William mused upon the idea. "Lady Pamela is, perhaps, more strong-willed than you think. Certainly, if her mother were to choose someone she had already settled upon, then I agree that things would go smoothly. But I cannot believe she would agree to marry anyone she had not developed a fondness for.

"Nor," he added, smiling to himself, "would her mother wish her to."

"Then you must make an effort to engage her affections, which is precisely my reason for confronting you this morning. You are talking in circles, William!"

"Am I? I do not mean to. It is you, it seems, who keeps confusing the matter. You spoke of my intended bride, and in the next breath you shifted to Lady Pamela."

By the rising color of his mother's cheeks, William judged that it was time to stop baiting her, even before Lady Westbury demanded, "William, you will stop playing games this instant and tell me what you mean!"

"Very happily, Mama. I am delighted to inform you that I have asked the Duchess of Upavon to be my wife."

"That . . . creature!" Lady Westbury so far forgot herself as to clap one hand to her pursed lips. "You are joking me, William, I know it. I have always deplored that tendency in you, but this time you try me too far!"

At her first words, William's brow had lowered, and now his jaw went rigid. "When Mathilda told me that she thought you would have reservations about the match, I did not credit her."

"Reservations! Have you entirely lost your memory, William? It is Lady Pamela who owns Westbury Manor, not her mother. Foolish boy! You have been wasting your time and have bungled the whole affair."

"*You* will be wasting my time if you mean to go on like this any longer." His warning was not entirely lost upon his mother, for she swallowed whatever she had been about to say. "You will wish, of course, to call upon my intended bride as soon as possible and make it clear how eagerly you welcome her into the family."

"I shall do no such thing! That woman is a hoyden! I am surprised that you have so little feeling for your mother as to try to foist her upon me."

"Doing it much too brown, Mama." William's

tone would brook no argument this time. "I suppose the source of your displeasure is in having your own plans overturned, but I would not mourn them overlong if I were you. I think Gerald will someday oblige you if you give him time enough to discover his own mind. But that is another issue, and none of our business, after all."

William paused and pretended to consider. "Perhaps it would be best if you did not call upon Mathilda immediately. Not until you have grown more comfortable with the notion, at any rate. I would prefer that she not be distressed by your lack of enthusiasm. When, however, I have judged the time is right, I shall take you to wait upon her myself."

Then, rising before she could issue any further protest, he said, "Now, if you will excuse me . . ." He circled his desk and assisted her from her chair. "I have one or two matters of business to attend. I shall see you at dinner."

Lady Westbury's body went rigid as he offered her his support. She refused to take his arm, and instead swept away from him and out the door.

*There,* William thought. The cat was out of the bag again before he could prevent it, but he still trusted in his ability to bring things about. He was used to handling his mother. Mattie was likely to be the more difficult of the two, no matter what she had said about being weak.

There was a firmness in her meekness, he had noticed before, almost as if the protective shell she had erected about her was as strong as iron.

"Well, we shall see," he said to himself. "Once

the news gets around—and now that my mother is in possession of it, it will be certain to do so—we shall see how that affects my Mattie."

the most perplexing and now that my mother
is in possession of it all, in certain to do
what she can now that we have any chance

# Chapter Ten

*M*attie's reaction came more quickly than
William could ever have imagined, for Lady
Westbury's words were related faithfully to her
by Mrs. Puckeridge. The rector's wife had the
good fortune to appear on her ladyship's doorstep
soon after her quarrel with William.

"She's a hoyden!" Lady Westbury exclaimed to
her visitor in red-faced indignation. "Nothing but
a hoyden to have set her cap at my son. Westbury had his eye, quite properly, on dear Lady
Pamela until that creature used some trickery to
snatch him from her own daughter."

Mrs. Puckeridge, who did not for one moment
believe that Lord Westbury had been tricked into
anything, still felt hurt that the duchess had
withheld the news of the engagement from her—
she, who was to have been her principal confidante.

"You say that the engagement will soon be
announced?" she asked, with the bitter taste of
gall invading her mouth.

Lady Westbury was only too glad to have
someone sympathetic to whom to pour out the
gross injustice of it all. "I suppose Westbury will
announce it, no matter what my feelings are

upon the subject. He has instructed me, if you please, to call upon Her Grace to welcome her into the family. But I have told him in no uncertain terms that I should rather die than do so."

"I can see why you would be hesitant," Mrs. Puckeridge commiserated. It was not often that Lady Westbury got her just deserts, so Mrs. Puckeridge could be forgiven a small feeling of satisfaction now. Her own sense of betrayal could be held responsible for the fact that its degree was so slight.

"You must be dreadfully disappointed that Westbury Manor will not be returned to the Norton patrimony."

Lady Westbury bristled, but she could not conceal the tenderest feature of her injury. "I had thought to have Westbury make it into my dower house. Norton Abbey is so drafty in winter. You would hardly credit how fiercely the chimneys smoke! And I bitterly resent seeing that woman cozily ensconced in a place that ought by all rights to have been mine."

Mrs. Puckeridge tut-tutted, but before her sympathy could have any lasting effect upon Lady Westbury's sensibilities, she added, "And now there is no possibility that the house will ever be yours. What a pity!"

Lady Westbury must have detected some degree of satisfaction in her visitor's voice, for she eyed her askance and quickly amended her story. "But, of course, my principal concern is for my son. How he could have proposed to a woman older than he, I cannot fathom! He could not be thinking of his inheritance. The Norton line has continued uninterrupted for centuries, and he must produce an heir."

"But surely the duchess is still of an age to bear him children?"

This reminder did nothing to smooth Lady Westbury's ruffled feathers. "No doubt she is," she conceded in spiteful accents, "but it would be quite improper for her to do so. Think of the tongues that will wag if she does! And I shall have to bear the mortification of it. I might as well take to my bed and declare myself an invalid, for all that I'll ever dare show my face in London again."

"Tsk-tsk," Mrs. Puckeridge murmured, perfectly aware that Lady Westbury never bestirred herself to travel as far as the metropolis under the best of circumstances. She took her leave presently, her wounded feelings only partially comforted by Lady Westbury's comeuppance.

Less than a day passed before she hurried to Westbury Manor to relate this conversation to the duchess. Mattie was first astonished, then hurt, to learn that William had announced their engagement as if it were a *fait accompli*.

"She called me a hoyden?" Mattie asked, an ache over William's betrayal momentarily overwhelming her other reactions. "But Lady Westbury is quite mistaken. I am not engaged to marry her son."

"No?" Mrs. Puckeridge showed signs of disappointment. "Lady Westbury seemed quite certain that you were."

"No, I most assuredly am not. I could not accept—that is, I could not think of marrying again, even if Lord Westbury did me the honor, which, of course, he did not."

Mattie felt a blush stealing painfully over her features as a result of this lie. She had not quite known how to respond to such impertinence. She had not had time to consider or to prepare for such a sudden confrontation.

The last twenty-four hours she had spent in an unhappy fog, never once thinking that William would spread the word that he had proposed.

Mrs. Puckeridge was eyeing her with distinct suspicion, as if some slip of the tongue had given away the true state of affairs.

Mattie drew herself up and said in her haughtiest tone, "Lady Westbury does me great wrong if she could suspect me of such evil intentions. And it wounds me greatly to think that a neighbor of mine—moreover, a lady who has been a guest in my house, who has sat in my parlor and drunk my sherry—could call me a hoyden!"

A strong sense of outrage had replaced her injury. What right did Mrs. Puckeridge have to bring her such unwelcome tidings?

"If you will excuse me," Mattie said, "I must get back to my duties. I must—"

You must leave, a quiet voice whispered in her ear. She must get away from all these spiteful people.

But where? A second voice challenged the first; but the first retorted, Go to Bath. Didn't Cosmo say he would be happy to have you visit him?

"I must pack," Mattie said to Mrs. Puckeridge, a quiet determination filling her with strength. "Pamela and I will be traveling tomorrow."

"Oh?" Mrs. Puckeridge perked up her ears at the news. "And where will you be going, if I may ask?"

"Of course you may," Mattie answered, smiling. She had no intention, however, of supplying the information her visitor wanted. "You must feel free to ask whatever you wish."

She rose then, and Mrs. Puckeridge had the grace to excuse herself with a hint of shame on her countenance. But Mattie was too distressed to derive any comfort from it.

*A hoyden!* she repeated to herself, as she climbed the stairs to Gilly's room. How dare Lady Westbury talk about her so!

By the time she had reached Gilly's door, however, Mattie had realized that she must not ask Gilly to commiserate with her. How could she tell her friend what had occurred without giving all away?

The thought that she had no one to turn to in her distress increased it, but Mattie did not mean to waver from her plan. She would go to Bath to escape the cruel tongues, which had already dared to invade her house. Then, once Lady Westbury saw that Mattie had no intention of marrying her son, she would be forgiven, and the whole affair would blow over.

But Mattie knew she must not take Gilly with her to Bath. Gilly would be stunned by the announcement that Mattie meant to travel without her, but Mattie would not be able to conceal her broken heart from her dearest friend in any other way.

With a sigh, she smoothed her dress and prepared to confront Gilly with the strange news.

William learned of Mattie's removal next morning when Gerald came into his library with a scowl on his face.

"What's the worry, bantling?" William coaxed him. "Lost some money on the horses? I warned you not to bet on Wilton's filly."

"No, it's not the horses," Gerald grumbled, throwing himself roughly into a chair. Its legs scraped the floor with a grating sound.

"Hold on," William warned him, hiding a budding concern behind a joking tone. "If you break that chair, our mother is likely to lock you in the cellar for a fortnight. Then you would miss all the schemes you've got planned."

"She might as well lock me in the cellar, though she would never do such a thing, and you know she wouldn't."

"Any why 'might as well'?"

"Because I've nothing to do anyway."

"Ah," William said on a long, drawn-out note. He pushed his chair back from his desk and propped up his booted feet. "Now we are getting somewhere. Why, so suddenly, are you bereft of all activity, when your face has hardly been seen in these parts for the past three weeks?"

Gerald's cheeks took on a ruddy tone. "You're exaggerating. Why, I've been here. As much as you ever are, anyway."

"Which is to say, hardly at all. I admit it freely. But we are straying from the point, and you have not answered my question. But—" William held up one hand as if to excuse himself "—you will say that I am damned impertinent to ask so many questions, and that I should be the last to insist on hearing all your secrets. So you may tell me to go to the devil, and I will try to take it in good part, although I should warn you at the outset that my feelings will be so injured, I just might slip into a decline."

This lengthy monologue at last drew a reluctant grin from his younger sibling. "Oh, very well," Gerald said, "though for pitching me so much gammon, I ought to wish you to the devil!"

His glance wandered to the floor, then to the hands in his lap, before he said in a mumble, "It's only that Lady Pam left home this morning—which wouldn't concern me in the least," he stressed, "only that we had planned a really capital ride, and then I was going to show her some drawings I'd made for her new stables, and since I'd mentioned only yesterday that I meant to do so, she might have told me that she planned to go. Don't you think?"

"Perhaps," William conceded, admirably concealing his amusement. He studied his fingernails. "It is always possible, however, that Lady Pamela did not anticipate her journey."

"Do you think so?" Gerald's eyes flew to William's face. "That's what I would have said, because she always acts so square with me. But—" he frowned "—don't you think it is rather odd of her mother to set out on a three-day journey—for do not think for a minute that John Coachman can make it in two—to set out like that without so much as a warning?"

"It does seem rather sudden."

When William appeared uncommunicative, disappointment gathered like a cloud over Gerald's features. He waited for his brother to speak, then shifted restlessly in his chair.

"I say, Will," he ventured after what seemed a considerable time, "you don't think Her Grace has any objection to my seeing Lady Pam so much?"

William heard the worry in his brother's voice and smiled. "You mean, does she think you plan to make off with her daughter, so she spirited her away?"

Gerald squirmed in his chair. "Nothing like that, no. At least—" he scoffed "—Lord, no, I hope not. It's only that I have been spending a great deal of time with her. And I might as well tell you that her groom doesn't always keep up with us—you know he's old, and we can't be expected to ride at a snail's pace, for Lord's sake! But," he stammered, "I started thinking that Her Grace might have got wind of it, and she might have worried that Pam—that Lady Pam was getting to be of an age when perhaps she ought not to go around unescorted. Not that I would ever do anything to hurt Pam!" he added ingenuously. "And anyway, she might have got worked up about it—quite beyond reason, mind you—and decided to take her away?"

William moved to put his brother at ease. "No need to worry, brat. I have a feeling that the duchess's mind has been on quite different matters. If she has given any thought to Lady Pamela and you, I suspect it has been very slight."

Relief washed over Gerald's face. "I don't see how you could know, but I hope you are right."

"Trust me," William said, hiding a smile. "I

take it that you and Lady Pamela are thick as thieves? And here I thought you had a low opinion of females."

Gerald grinned and tried not to flush again, but the color had already begun creeping up his neck. "Well, she is a different sort of girl. . . ."

"Precisely what I told you from the first, if you recall," William said. Then, seeing how greatly his brother was discomfited, he dropped the point and asked instead, "I do not suppose you were told where she was going?"

"No, not at first. But I managed to wring it out of Tim—her groom, you know." Gerald's look of determination was followed by one of pure disgust. "You will think I am trying to humbug you, Will, but would you believe it? Pam's mother has dragged her to Bath!"

William laughed in a sudden burst of delight, which was only due in part to his brother's face. "Of course I believe it. Where else would Mattie go but the one place she could be guaranteed to be surrounded by octogenarians?" He leaned back in his chair and enjoyed the mental picture this occasioned.

After a moment, seeing that Gerald was looking blue again, he offered, "How would you like to join me on a trip?"

Gerald only brightened slightly. "A trip? To where?"

"To Bath, of course. What other place have we been discussing?"

"To Bath? You and me?" A ludicrous aspect, part pleasure, part bewilderment, came over Gerald's face. "But you just said— You know, Will, Bath is devilish flat."

"So it is said. But perhaps it only needs a little stirring up. Shall we go?"

Doubt clouded Gerald's gaze. "I don't know. . . . What'll we do for sport?"

"I have my own prey in mind, but I daresay you and Lady Pam will find a ride or two worthy of your consideration."

"Will you let me take Jupiter?" Gerald asked, scooting to the edge of his seat. "And another mount for Pam? You must know how she despises hacks."

"You may take whichever horses you want, although not the entire stable, I beg of you. I might have need of them myself one day."

"Ah, Will, don't be such a ninnyhammer." Gerald's eyes might have lighted the stage at Covent Garden. "But now that I think about it, I know there is one stud worth seeing that's not too far from Bath. And I could take my drawings to show Pam."

"That's the spirit. I shall inform the servants directly, if you would be so kind as to take the message to our mother." William reached for the bell. "And by the way, you might omit to mention that we expect to see our neighbors there."

Gerald grinned as he leapt to his feet. "I might be a dunderhead, but I'm not so green as that!"

"Are you not?" His brother smiled after him. "Then I can see that Lady Pamela has exerted a most beneficial effect, indeed."

After Gerald had left, William pondered for a moment, realizing that he could not have planned a more fortunate change in circumstance. Mattie had fled, but what she had fled to was exactly what she needed to show her the brevity of the world's memory and the fickleness of society.

William had planned to prove to her that he could protect her from the worst of society's arrows. He had thought he could persuade her to marry him eventually, and had envisioned with eagerness the form that persuasion would take. But how much better it would be, he told himself now, if Mattie could learn for herself the futility of seeking approval from persons whose one pleasure in life was to destroy the happiness of others.

His Mattie would need the freedom to learn those lessons that ought to have been mastered at an earlier age. William could exercise patience, even though the urge to hold her almost overpowered him at times. He would go to Bath to oversee her tutoring and take the pleasure of watching his English rose unfurl her soft petals, making sure, of course, to be ready when the moment came to catch them up.

If Gerald could have witnessed Pamela's journey to Bath, he would have seen that the aspersions he had cast upon her driver were fully justified. Even Mattie, who was used to moving at a snail's pace, grew frustrated with their progress.

"Do you think we might urge the horses to go a little faster?" she asked John Coachman on the second day of their journey, when it seemed as if they might never arrive.

She was rewarded with a scowl. "Ye never told

me ye was in no hurry, Miss Mattie." John Coachman bristled with her interference.

"It is not that I am in a hurry—" Mattie hastened to soothe his feelings "—for I most assuredly am not. It is just that we seem to be moving a touch more slowly than our custom, and I thought that perhaps the horses might be persuaded to step up their pace a little."

"If there's no need to spring 'em, and I guess ye've growed used to such fancy goers that ye don't rightly recall the proper pace for a lady, then ye'd best let me go about my work the way I knows it best."

"Of course, you must. And, of course, there is no need to spring them. Whyever would there be? I have no need to hurry." Mattie decided to give up trying. She could tell by John's expression that her suggestion would have the reverse effect of what she had desired. Now she would be lucky indeed to make Bath in only three days. Insisting upon speed would only put up his hackles to the point that he might stop for a few days to nurse some imagined injury to one of the horses' legs.

In the shadows of her mind was an image of William, riding after them and forcing her to return to face his mother. Mattie could not forget the determined look that had settled upon his face. She could only imagine what he would do when he learned of her sudden departure, but she had instructed Barlow to withhold her destination from him.

Knowing how arrogant William could be, how competent and beautifully masterful, she had no illusions of having bought herself much time. But Coachman would drive so slowly!

Now that Mattie had interfered, he took twice as long to climb back onto the box. And his "herrup" was so dispirited that at first the horses could not even hear it, and Mattie was obliged to bite her tongue until he flicked their backs with the reins.

At last their procession was under way. In her whole life, Mattie had never been in such a hurry. She wanted to hide herself among the townspeople of Bath, and for once, felt no fright at the prospect.

It would be much worse, far much worse, to face her neighbors, particularly Lady Westbury, with the announcement that William had proposed.

By carefully shielding her impatience, Mattie had hoped to overcome her setback with John, but if she was chafed by their slowness, her daughter was in torture. More than once, Pamela expressed so much frustration that she actually begged her mother to let her drive them herself.

"Nonsense, my dear," Mattie finally chided her. "You know very well you can do no such thing. If you will not think of Coachman's feelings, think of your own reputation if it were to leak out that you had shoved your servant aside to do his job."

Pamela was sulking in the corner of the carriage, which was not at all like her. "If we do have to go to Bath, we might as well get there."

"Don't you want to go, dearest?" Concern chased other thoughts from Mattie's head. She had been so possessed by worries of her own, she had failed to notice Pamela's reluctance, but now she could not miss it. "Are you worried about being in an unfamiliar place? Among a new set of people?"

Pamela stared at her mother as if she had suddenly spouted Greek. "What?"

Mattie colored. "It is only that if you have such fears, I am sure they are quite natural, but you mustn't let them come to dominate you. I feel quite certain that we will be welcomed in Bath. You must not forget that Cosmo is there. He will have friends he can present to us, and some of them will surely have children your age. You must not let their newness frighten you."

"Oh. That." With this puzzling response, Pamela settled back in her corner and stared unhappily out the window.

For the rest of the trip, Mattie did her best to squelch Pamela's irritation, with the result that John Coachman brought them to Bath at last. He pulled up the horses in front of the duke's impressive residence on the Royal Crescent.

Shuttered windows and a door from which the knocker had been removed greeted their eyes.

With a sinking heart, Mattie asked John Coachman to rouse the house, but the result was predictable. The servant who answered expressed his regret, but said that the duke had gone into Wiltshire to visit a friend and would not be back for three weeks. He was certain His Grace would wish for beds to be made up for his visitors at once, if they would wish to come inside, but he warned them that the staff had been given a holiday, so they might not find things exactly as they wished.

Mattie's heart filled with dismay. She hardly knew what to say, she was so dumbfounded, but she could not bring herself to impose on the few of Cosmo's servants who had remained.

"I thought you said Uncle Cosmo would be here?" Pamela asked. Her tone was surprisingly indifferent for one who must have been feeling anxious about the trip.

"I thought he would be. He said he was just on his way back when he spent the evening at Westbury Manor, and I never thought he would leave again so soon. . . ." Mattie's heart was fluttering, but she knew she must not let her own trepidation raise fears in her daughter's breast.

"Well," she said purposefully, as if this sort of setback occurred daily in her life, "we shall just have to put up at an inn. Then perhaps we can find lodgings of our own. In fact, I am sure we can."

But she was not so certain. Mattie had left Westbury Manor with no other plan in mind than to flee William's notice and the rumors that were sure to abound when Mrs. Puckeridge spread her gossip. She had not brought her dresser, for Turner could not be expected to make such a long journey at her age. And naturally, presuming that she would find Cosmo at home, she had left all her other servants behind. She could not possibly set up house without them.

There would be nothing for it. They would have to return with their tails between their legs and another failure added to her other shames, but for the moment, everyone was tired and they must have a decent night's sleep.

She told John Coachman to drive them to an inn, hoping that his memory could dredge up a place of lodging that would still be standing after so many years.

To her infinite gratitude, he did. The White Lion in Market Place, where His Grace had been used to stay as a younger man, was not only standing, but bustling with activity, and although it did not have the air of being the first in its class, it appeared much more than respectable.

Mattie worried that the bustle might be a signal that the rooms had all been taken, but the innkeeper, upon seeing a dignified carriage entering his gate, hurried to welcome them. A word from John Coachman as to who his passengers were, and the man was all bows.

"It's the Catch Club, Your Grace," he explained, letting down the step for her. "They meets here during the winter, and some of the gentlemen likes to sit in my taproom the whole year round. I hope their singing won't disturb you."

He seemed so anxious to please that Mattie felt her flutterings die away. She smiled and assured Mr. Arnold that she would greatly enjoy the sound of voices raised in an occasional glee.

It was the truth. Mattie could not be quite so anxious when such avid propounders of musical science were filling the rooms with harmony. And inside, the White Lion proved to be quite elegant.

"Tomorrow," Mattie said bravely to Pamela, as they made their way up the creaking stairs, "we shall buy ourselves a guidebook and explore the town."

# Chapter Eleven

*M*attie did find a guidebook the next afternoon, but not before many surprising and pleasant things had occurred.

She was awakened in the morning by a cheerful maid who brought chocolate to her in bed. Then, she had no sooner dressed with this girl's help than she was served the most delicious breakfast imaginable in a quiet parlor Mr. Arnold had reserved for her and Pamela.

"Your Grace didn't say nothing about taking my best room, but I took the liberty of holding it back for you, thinking you might be more cozy-like in here."

"That was most kind of you," Mattie replied, and indeed, she was more than a little grateful to him. The singers' voices had been pleasant, but she was not at all certain she would have wanted to sit in a crowded taproom, surrounded by a group of strange men.

This private parlor was the sort of thing an experienced traveler would have known how to speak for directly, and Mattie was afraid that Mr. Arnold would hold her in disgust for not knowing any better.

"You see," she explained hesitantly, "my daughter and I had planned to stay with her uncle, His Grace of Upavon, but we arrived to find his house closed up."

At Mr. Arnold's curious look, she hastened to cover her mistake. "My letter, warning him of our arrival, must have missed him, but since that was my intention, I have not brought my servants with me."

"Ah, I see, Your Grace." Mr. Arnold smiled without a trace of suspicion. "I couldn't help but see that your maid was not with you. That's why I sent our Betty up to your room. I hope she satisfied."

"Oh, yes, indeed!" Mattie could breathe easily now that he had accepted her facile explanation. Feeling much better as a result, she just had to ask, "This marmalade, Mr. Arnold. It is so good, you must tell me where you procured it." As she spoke, Mattie spooned another thick dollop upon the fresh bread that had accompanied her bacon and eggs.

Mr. Arnold accepted the compliment with a bow and a flush of pride. "That's what the missus puts by, and she'll be that glad to know you liked it. I'm sure she'd be happy to give you the receipt. I can send her in, if you like."

"Yes, I would like that enormously." Mattie watched him bow himself out, reflecting sadly that even if she managed to get the receipt, Cook would surely not be persuaded to try it. Not that she would refuse, but she would say how much her ankles hurt if she stood too long at the stove, which putting up preserves would necessarily require, and the long and short of it would be that Mattie would end by revoking her request.

Reflections like these, and the novel sensation of being out on her own, occupied her mind her first morning in Bath, so that she did not have much time to brood about William. Mrs. Arnold was pleased that Mattie liked her cooking, and both she and her husband seemed anxious to make Mattie's stay comfortable.

But these people must not know about the scandal of my first marriage, Mattie told herself. Or if they did, they were not in a position to hold it against her. It was the ton who would remember and not forgive.

Mattie was in her room, bracing herself to face them on a walk about the town before returning home, when she received a visitor.

The name on his card meant nothing to her until Mr. Arnold informed her that the gentleman asking to see her was none other than Master of the Ceremonies of the Upper Assembly Rooms. It seemed that Mr. Arnold, pleased to be entrusted with such an important visitor, had sent a boy to notify Mr. King of her arrival in their town.

"I knew he would want to know right away that Your Grace was here," Mr. Arnold said, surprising Mattie completely.

She almost asked why, but then remembered she had been married to a duke and that she was a duchess.

"You may show him into the parlor," she said, wiping her damp palms upon her skirt. Mattie took a quick look in the glass upon her dressing table to make sure her hair was not a mess. She could be glad for the gown from Madame Riviere, for she had nothing to be anxious about in her dress.

When she entered the little parlor, a well-starched gentleman rose and extended her his deepest bow.

"Your Grace." His white hat, so peculiar in color, nearly scraped the floor. "I hope I do not intrude upon you too early in the day."

As it was nearly noon, and Mattie was used to being up and out long before this hour, she could only stammer, "Not at all. In fact, I was on the point of going out."

Thinking that perhaps these words did not convey her pleasure to receive his call, she amended them with, "To find a guidebook and explore your delightful city."

Mr. King beamed at the compliment, as if he and not the celebrated architect Mr. John Wood were responsible for the elegant buildings to be found here. He begged her to take a chair and held one for her, then asked if he might be so bold as to join her.

"Certainly." Mattie suppressed a smile. The man was so obsequious, and yet so self-important, as to raise a bubble of mirth even in her untutored head.

Once he was seated, she expressed her surprise over his visit.

"Ah, Your Grace understands the burdens upon my time." Mr. King spoke with a sigh. "You must have seen at a glance that the great extension of our city makes it impossible for me to be regularly informed of the several persons who arrive here, but a visitor of your distinction must surely be greeted or you would have just cause to complain of a want of attention. Mr. Arnold is to be commended for calling your arrival to my notice, else I might have made the error, through no intention of mine, I assure you, of neglecting Your Grace in favor of a person of lesser importance."

"I see," Mattie said, and she began to see, in fact, that she was regarded by some, at least, to be vastly important. The fact that her position as a dowager duchess was entirely responsible did not lessen her relief, not when her fear of being rejected had been so high.

Perhaps the scandal about her marriage was so old that she would not be cut as she had feared. Or maybe the ton had had time to forgive her perceived mistake, given the quiet nature of her behavior since.

Then Pamela would be all right. But Mattie swore she would do nothing to arouse the enmity of society now, such as marrying a man younger than she who must be regarded as one of its greatest prizes.

At the thought of William, her heart filled with lead, but she did not allow her visitor to see her sorrow. She smiled and nodded while Mr. King described to her the amusements of the Upper Rooms, which, under any other circumstances, would have sounded delightful.

But she had forgotten that she could not stay in Bath.

When Mr. King paused to gather breath, Mattie took the opportunity to say, "I am certain my daughter and I would enjoy your assemblies, and I myself came with the intention of taking the waters, but I am afraid we cannot stay." She proceeded to the same story she had given Mr. Arnold.

After only a brief pause, Mr. King offered a polite protest. "But surely Your Grace could hire a house?"

"Yes, but—"

"You need not think it will be too difficult. With such a continual succession of arrivals and departures, a lodging suitable to every wish is generally quite easy to find."

"Yes, I would, you see, but—" Mattie flushed to admit her incompetence "—if only I had brought my servants with me, but . . ."

"I understand perfectly, Your Grace." Mr. King inclined his head. "With such excellent servants as you naturally possess, one would hesitate to accept the services of—shall we say—a lesser-trained sort. But I can assure Your Grace that here in Bath you will find a number of qualified persons as would suit your purposes quite adequately for an indefinite stay. In fact—"

Mr. King drew a card from his pocket and handed it to Mattie. "If I might suggest . . . the name here is that of a superior agency for recommending just that sort of individual Your Grace might require." Then a different notion seemed to enter his mind, for he added, "But . . . if I might be permitted . . . ?"

Mattie nodded, ready to permit Mr. King anything so long as he would not expect her to call upon the agency and engage an entire household of new servants.

He continued, "I have just been put in mind of a house that might be not only available, but could be taken with its full complement of servants. Lady Findlay—but perhaps you know her?"

Mattie did not.

"A charming lady, if I might be permitted to say. In any case, her ladyship resides in Bath the year around because of the healthful benefit of our waters. But," he added, "due to the persistent nature of her complaint, I am afraid her medical man has prescribed a different cure, and she has left us to tour the Lake Country for the season, taking—since her purposes are related to health and only temporary in nature—only her maid and coachman."

Mattie followed this embellished tale to its end, and then asked timidly, "What you are saying is that perhaps Lady Findlay could be persuaded to let me use her house for the remainder of the season? A house for which no additional servants would be required?"

"Precisely, Your Grace, with the exception of a maid for yourself, of course, for which task the agency I have suggested to you might safely be applied. And if you would permit me to act as intermediary, I am certain her ladyship would be more than delighted at the arrangement."

Mattie sat and reflected upon the daring notion of taking a house for the season—all on her own.

The servants would be strangers. Besides John Coachman, there would be no one familiar to her. She would have to face them all and learn their idiosyncrasies.

But wasn't that why she had come to Bath? To get away from everyone at home? Anyone who knew her and might guess that she had nearly embarrassed herself and that her heart had been broken?

She would have to hire a maid, for no duchess would establish herself in town and then dress herself.

With a disloyal thrill, she thought of how much fun it might be to buy more new dresses and have an eager, youthful soul around to rave over each one. With such new experiences to cheer her, she might even be able to forget for a minute or two how much she missed William. She might even offer the position—temporarily, of course— to Mr. Arnold's cheerful daughter.

"How soon do you think you might get a response from Lady Findlay?" she asked Mr. King.

"By return mail," he answered promptly. "I have taken it upon myself to perform a few slight services on her ladyship's behalf, since her departure was so sudden. As a result, we have been in frequent communication, and since I believe I know what her mind will be upon this subject, you might consider the agreement as having already been made."

He smiled roguishly, with the air of a man who would expect a return for his services. "And I hope this will mean we might expect your delightful presence at our assemblies?"

All had been concluded so fast that Mattie suddenly found herself breathless, and unable to speak, she simply nodded accord to what moments before had seemed an impossibility.

She had taken a house. She and Pamela, in no more than a few days, would be living in a place they had never seen, surrounded by strangers, and Mattie herself would be mistress of the entire establishment. It was almost more than she could believe, but it was exactly what was needed. This way, she would not have to face either William, or Lady Westbury, or Mrs. Puckeridge, or even Gilly again, until she had recovered from her broken heart.

After discovering the duke's house closed and inquiring at all the inns, William traced his prey to Lady Findlay's house quite easily. He applauded Mattie's industry in finding a suitable lodging on her own and the courage that had led her to do it. William decided, however, not to threaten her by appearing on her doorstep, but instead frequented the places in which he thought he might see her.

In Bath, this would be quite simple. Every person of rank, resident and visitor alike, could be expected to make an appearance in the Pump-room in the mornings. After an interval of a decent number of days, by which time he hoped Mattie would have got her feet on the ground, and during which he helped Gerald exercise their horses, William strolled from his room at the White Hart in Stall Street to the nearby Pump-room.

He saw her immediately, sitting near a Corinthian column in the midst of a group of elderly gentlemen, who seemed quite intent on securing her attention. William smiled to see how quickly she had gained a circle of admirers, and he determined to become one of them. He looked about the large room, hoping to spot an acquaintance who could perform an introduction.

He was not long in finding one. An aged friend

of his father's, who walked with a cane, had taken a place near the door. Sir Reginald Pursey gladly greeted his old crony's son in a rather loud voice.

"Westbury, my boy! What brings you to this ghastly place? Not taking the waters, I hope, like the rest of us?" Sir Reginald made a face over the glass in his hand. "Vile stuff! But they say it does wonders for the gout, so I'm condemned to try it." Another thought seized him. "Not attending your mother, are you?"

"No, sir. Just visiting." William allowed his gaze to wander back to where Mattie was holding court and said, "I thought you might be able to tell me who that ravishing creature is."

"Ain't she?" Sir Reginald's eyes had followed William's and located Mattie with little effort. "She's the Duchess of Upavon, my lad, and now we know why the old codger kept her to himself. Though they do say he was never one for society." He cocked an eye toward William, who did nothing to hide his admiration of Mattie's beauty. "Thinking of having a go at the dowager, are you?"

"If I can get myself introduced. Would you do the honors?"

Sir Reginald barked a laugh. "I have got that far, at least, though you've got to be a mite faster than me on this damned stick to get close to that one. And don't think I haven't tried. Why, if I were just ten years younger—"

"And unmarried, I presume . . ." William hastened to cut off his confidence.

"Don't think it for a moment." Sir Reginald winked at him, then poked him in the ribs with his cane. "Give me your arm, boy, and I'll use this to clear us a path.

"Nasty old buggers," he mumbled loudly, as they reached the crowd surrounding Mattie. "Not a one of 'em under ninety. Ought to be ashamed of themselves."

William hid his grin at this gross exaggeration. He was doing his best to appear as if he had never met Mattie before. But he found this almost impossible when the group parted between them and her eyes met his.

The look upon her face nearly proved his undoing. First she turned pale, and than a rosy pink. A pulse beat rapidly at her throat, just above the spot he had so recently kissed.

"Lord—" The trembling word escaped her lips before William interrupted, turning to Sir Reginald.

"Sir, will you present me?"

"My dear ..." In his loudest voice, Sir Reginald had already sprung to the task, enjoying the superior age that allowed him to be so familiar with her. "This young gentleman has begged me to make him known to you. As a suitor, I can recommend him highly, seeing as how his papa and I were friends, don't you know. He is Westbury."

During this speech, which was loud enough for all in the room to hear, Mattie had recovered much of her composure. Now, with only a little tremble, she was able to hold out her hand for William to take.

He did so, bowing to kiss it and resisting the temptation to linger over it. "Your Grace."

"My lord ..." Mattie snatched back her hand

and buried it in her lap, beneath her reticule and book.

William was happy to see that she was still trembling. "Have you been here long, duchess?"

She glanced at him, seemingly unsure of the game he was playing, but William knew perfectly well what he was about. This time he meant to court her publicly. No more hiding for either of them.

"I have been here but a week."

"I, too. And do you find Bath to your liking?"

Now she was surprised. She was probably wondering why he had not tracked her down before.

"Yes indeed." Mattie fanned herself, though the room was rather chilly. "Yes, I like Bath very much."

"And how long do you plan to stay?"

"Through the season. I have taken a house," she said, stressing the last word in the way one might say one had climbed a mountain.

"So I have heard." When she raised her eyebrows in question, he added, "I, on the other hand, do not plan to take a house, but I find myself quite comfortably settled for the season at the White Hart, which is no more than a stroll from here."

"But why?" The words escaped her before she considered. "Surely you cannot wish to spend the entire summer at Bath?"

"And why not? Did we not just agree that it is charming?" William smiled at her obvious distress. "Besides, I have a purpose in coming here."

"You do?" Her voice was small.

"Yes, I came to find a particular person, a connection that seemed quite lost to me, but one which I am determined to recover."

"Oh." Now she sounded breathless, but there was nothing she could say to discourage him, not with so many men around.

After a moment, she thought of something. "I have come to take the waters," she emphasized. "Like other people of an advanced age, I find I am in need of more immediate medical advice."

At the outrageous claim of age, a chuckle went up amongst her courtiers.

"What's that? What did she say?" one gentleman asked, and another repeated for him the duchess's delightful joke.

Doing it much, much too brown, William told her with his eyes, and Mattie had the grace to flush. But she had given him his opening. "Then perhaps you would stroll with me to the fountain, where we both might sample a drink?"

Before she could refuse him, he took a step closer and proffered his arm, willing her to come with him.

Drawn by his compelling look, Mattie took his arm before she had time to think. The feel of steel beneath her palm caused her pulse to jump.

The gentlemen in her retinue must have felt William's superior claim, for they faded away as if in one body.

"William, you shouldn't have come," she whispered to him as they cleared the small group. "It is pointless."

"Surely not pointless. I meant what I said, Mattie. I mean to convince you, so naturally I had to find you."

"But you cannot!"

"If I cannot, then you have nothing to worry about. And if I can, then we both may be happy. So don't let my presence disturb you. Just ignore me. Treat me like some annoying fly. With so many suitors, it is certainly your prerogative."

A giggle welled up inside her, and she felt her cheeks warming. "They are not my suitors," she said, though she knew they very well were. It had been a new experience to have the attention of so many men. New, and not altogether displeasing.

At first Mattie had thought they were only being kind to her. Then she had noticed the admiration in their eyes, a sight she might not have recognized if she had not first seen it in William's. At the thought of William, all her pleasure had diminished, for none of the men could touch her heart as he had.

Reacting belatedly to his last comment, she said, "And treat you like a fly, William? Do not be absurd. You must know I could not do that."

"Then you do love me, and you had better face it and come live with me, my love."

Mattie did her best to squelch the inevitable feelings of pain and pleasure his words aroused. By now, they had reached the alcove where a fountain spewed water from several openings into a great marble basin.

"I am far too old for marriage," she said. "All this furor has overset me, and I do need a cure." To prove this to him, she turned to the attendant and asked for a dipper of the waters.

"How much is it, please?" she said, raising her reticule.

"Shame on you, Mattie." William took the cup

and served her himself before pulling a coin from his pocket and pressing it into the attendant's palm. "Do you mean to say," he asked, turning toward her as she raised the cup to her lips, "that you have been here a whole week and have not yet tasted the waters? I thought you were here on a cure?"

Mattie flushed under his teasing gaze just as a mouthful of warm, brackish water assaulted her tongue. It was all she could do not to spit it out.

William laughed at the look on her face. "Don't you care for it? You had much better let me serve you champagne, Mattie. You should always drink champagne."

The beautiful vision his words conjured up was so tempting, Mattie felt her knees begin to quake. "I have not taken the waters because I have not yet consulted a physician, but I will as soon as possible. I have not been well."

She would be firm with William, she told herself. She would be firm, and when he saw that she was determined in her refusal, he would go away. Or, much better yet, he would ask her to be his mistress after all.

Only why, she thought as she turned back towards the room and saw several people staring at them speculatively, why did he have to pursue her in public? He might have come to her house under cover of darkness when she could have kissed him instead, and no one the wiser.

This naughty thought surprised her and told her she must strengthen her resolve.

"Where is Pamela?" William asked quickly, as Mr. Pickering—a new admirer, rather short and perky—perceived her across the room and started toward them.

Mattie had smiled to welcome the older man, whose presence would put a stop to this distressing interview, but at the mention of Pamela's name, she recalled the touch of anxiety she had experienced that morning.

"My daughter," she said, feigning a distance from William as soon as Mr. Pickering was close enough to hear them, "is here with me in Bath. I had hoped she would join me on my walk this morning, and indeed, she was on the point of doing so when she suddenly developed the headache. I would have stayed with her—" Mattie turned to William, unable to keep herself from admitting her concern to him "—but she insisted upon staying behind alone. She *said* she would *read*."

This behavior had been so unlike Pamela as to worry Mattie, who, wrapped in her own sorrows, had not noticed until that morning that Pamela had not acted herself since their arrival in Bath. Normally cheerful and energetic, she had seemed increasingly dull and listless.

All this, Mattie would have liked to confide to William, except that Mr. Pickering had reached them, and with a look much like a bantam rooster itching for a fight, was waiting to be presented.

Mattie performed the introduction, wishing that Mr. Pickering would take himself off, so she could hear William's thoughts about Pamela. Then, realizing the uncharitableness of her wish—seeing as how, with a smile, she had invited the man to join them—she smiled even more warmly upon him. William's courtesy matched her own, but a softening in his eye told her that he sympathized with her anxiety.

After a few moments of innocuous chat, William turned and said, "Duchess, I have brought my younger brother with me, and if you permit, he would like to call upon your daughter. He has brought a mount, and if you would let me lend Lady Pamela my own, there are some lovely rides across the hills around Bath."

"Oh!" *Gerald is here*—Mattie caught herself before she cried it aloud. "That would be just the thing. I think she has been missing her horses."

She knew that Pamela had developed a great friendship with Gerald. Perhaps she was missing her friends.

To Mattie, who had never had a chance to develop friendships, this was a new concept, but during her past week in Bath, she had missed William so much, she had been given a new understanding of such things.

William was smiling at her now with that familiar teasing twist to his lips that made her want to cry.

Mr. Pickering interrupted, saving her from the embarrassment of doing so. "Duchess, may I procure a glass of the waters for you?"

The prospect of drinking another sip of the foul stuff under William's eye made her stammer, "No, thank you, sir. I think I should consult my physician before drinking too much of the waters for my particular condition."

"To look at you, duchess," Mr. Pickering said, sweeping her a bow in the most courtly fashion, "one would think you in the pink of health."

"Yes, wouldn't one?" William agreed wickedly. "One would find it almost impossible to believe that she could have anything at all the matter with her."

"Well, I do," Mattie said, surprising Mr. Pickering with her defiant tone. Out of William, she got nothing but a falsely sympathetic look that a simpleton could see through.

And, of course, she was lying, but how dare he think he could shame her into owning it. Mattie would have made some reference to the aches and pains of age if her last attempt had not been greeted with such amusement. But she must make William see that even if she was not very old, strictly speaking, she was not of an appropriate age to be his wife.

Let him see what these others would say if they only suspected her of loving him.

This thought made her sick with anxiety. She felt truly pale. "I think I had best get home to Pamela."

Mr. Pickering seemed disappointed, but he bowed and moved aside to let her pass.

William bowed, too, but he offered her his arm to walk her to the door. She could not refuse him without appearing churlish.

Mr. Pickering hesitated in midbow as if he had just caught himself in a mistake. He took a step in front of them. "Shall we see you at the assembly this evening, Your Grace? You and your charming daughter?"

For all the world, Mattie would not have wanted William to be by her side at that moment. She had promised Mr. King to attend the assembly, but she did not want William to know.

"That will depend upon the health of my daughter," she replied, thinking that Pamela might provide her with an excuse. "If she has not recovered from her headache, we shall have to miss it."

William said, "I have taken a subscription to the Upper Rooms that includes two additional tickets for ladies only. I would be honored if you would accept them from me, Your Grace."

Mattie faltered. But . . . she couldn't. What would people say if she did? Why, Mr. Pickering was looking daggers at William already, just at the suggestion.

"That is very kind of you, Wil—Lord Westbury, but I have already procured tickets for the season."

"You have?" As William swept her past Mr. Pickering with a slight nod, he seemed anything but downcast. "Then I shall be certain of seeing you some nights there, shall I not? I shall have to tell my brother, Gerald. He is very fond of dancing."

Mattie was at pains not to laugh at this outrageous lie, which had clearly been designed to undermine her dignity. "William," she whispered as they walked toward the door, "I will not dance with you, so you must not even think it."

"No?" He tsked. "It is a pity, but you know, I think we should only waltz together—it is much more intimate—and no one is allowed to waltz in Bath. That is why it is so devilish flat."

Mattie felt an absurd giggle burgeoning inside her again. Why, oh, why did William have to be so charming?

She knew she would have to consult a physician and get him to prescribe the most disgusting cure, so that William would be brought to think she was too infirm to marry him.

# Chapter Twelve

*That* night at the assembly, Mattie and Pamela sat in the chairs reserved for peeresses—Pamela all in white, as befitted her age, and Mattie in a soft gray gown and a white cap, which she insisted befitted hers. They watched the dancers perform their dainty steps out on the dance floor. On Mattie's left, a gaunt Lady Repton in a mauve turban ran a constant commentary upon the ladies and gentlemen who swept before them.

"That is Lady Whitmore's niece," she said, making no attempt to conceal the object of her discourse. "Twenty-eight years if she's a day, and still on the shelf. Her parents have brought her down from London in the hope she will catch a more elderly suitor before they give her up for lost."

Mattie hardly knew how to reply to such an ungenerous speech, but Lady Repton's other neighbor faced her with more courage.

"Pooh!" Mrs. Dempling said across her. "Likely the girl is more particular than most, which she has every right to be." Mrs. Dempling was a kindly woman, prettily plump in spite of her graying hair, which led Mattie to believe she had had a fair share of suitors in her day.

"No, you are mistaken," Lady Repton pronounced. "Her mother confided her circumstances to me. The girl has received not even one proposal."

"A fine thing for her mother to put about! Tell the world that she's getting desperate? Might as well hold an ax over the girl's head. Clearly, she's so nervous, they've nearly chased the life out of the child."

"Child?" Lady Repton insisted upon having the last word. "One could hardly call her a child. Why, by her age, I was married and had six children."

Poor dears, Mattie thought to herself. She noted Mrs. Dempling's shrewd expression and fancied a similar thought had run through her mind. Mrs. Dempling's eye met Mattie's across her ladyship's bony chest, and she winked.

"Well," Mrs. Dempling said, scanning the dance floor and changing the subject of their dissection. "She has a superior partner in Mr. Warrenton."

Lady Repton sniffed. "A widower, saddled with three troublesome children, or so I have heard them described. Hardly a prize catch in my book."

Mattie and Mrs. Dempling exchanged another look. A dimple peeking out from the other woman's cheek nearly caused Mattie to break into a giggle, so she turned away before lapsing into subdued silence.

When no one responded to her last remark, Lady Repton cast a glance Pamela's way and demanded to know, "Will your daughter be dancing this evening, Your Grace?"

"I think not," Mattie said, fearful of what Lady Repton might say if Pamela did. "She is not yet out."

Her ladyship permitted herself a tight, approving smile. "I applaud your restraint, which, alas, in these days, is so seldom seen. But, of course, girls with dowries the size of Lady Pamela's rarely need help in finding adequate dance partners. It is the parents with so little with which to endow who feel they must push their daughters upon the world."

Her maternal instincts aroused, Mattie turned to Pamela to see how she had borne this rude comment, but Pamela did not seem to have heard it. She was sitting on the edge of her seat, scanning the room for new arrivals.

Since receiving a visit from Gerald that afternoon, Pamela had completely recovered from her indisposition and had looked forward to tonight's entertainment with barely concealed excitement. She had even submitted to the crimping of her curls with little protest. Mattie was too relieved to see her daughter in high spirits to question too deeply the cause of such a rapid recovery. Pamela's heightened color had all the welcome look of good health.

Mattie herself had not been at home when Gerald called, apparently without William. She had been sitting in Number 29, The King's Circus, consulting with an eminent physician, Fellow of the Royal Society, and Member of the Royal College of Physicians.

The elegant Dr. Falconer had asked for several

details about her symptoms, and Mattie was glad she had taken the trouble to provide herself with a list: lowness of spirit; loss of appetite. She had tried to think of others, but in the end had shied away from most. Claims of stomachache, which would be grossly untrue, might lead to too close an examination. Having never been ill, aside from an occasional cold, she was not certain just what a doctor did in more particular cases, and she certainly did not want to invite a search that might uncover her deceit.

Consequently, she played it safe by describing her general symptoms since William's arrival in Bath. And, if the doctor peered at her a bit strangely when nothing more serious was forthcoming than a deplorable tendency to stare morosely into thin air, at least he never accused her of making false claims. He prescribed a modest cure, of which a change in regime seemed the principal ingredient, and—she was particularly grateful for this part—no more than two dippers of the waters per day.

Now that her "illness" had been certified by a physician, Mattie hoped William would see that she indeed was suffering from the complaints of advanced age. He had not yet made an appearance tonight, but Mattie was certain Pamela would alert her to his arrival in time to compose herself.

Lady Repton's insistence upon sitting next to her had taken Mattie by surprise. She had not expected to be acknowledged by such a haughty member of the ton. But Lady Repton proved to be a virtual encyclopedia when it came to family connections and claimed to have a distant relative who had married into Mattie's own family.

"You were a Delacorte, were you not, before marrying the duke?" Lady Repton had asked soon after taking her chair.

"Yes. My father was Sir Geoffrey Delacorte."

Lady Repton inclined her head, as if Mattie had confirmed one of her most profoundly held notions. "My mother's great-uncle," she supplied, with an air of great wisdom, "had a first cousin who married into that branch of the Delacortes. She would have been your grandfather's great-aunt. A most distinguished woman. Perhaps you heard your parents speak of her?"

"No, I am afraid I did not." Mattie was sure that Lady Repton would consider it a great fault in her not to have heard of such an august personage. "But, you see, they both died when I was young." She shrank inwardly, waiting for her inquisitor to recall the circumstance of her marriage.

But Lady Repton, as poisonous as her mind could be upon certain topics, only replied, "Yes, I remember the story now. A boating accident, was it not?"

"Yes."

"I remember that my father read us the article about it when it occurred. The same piece mentioned that you had gone to live as His Grace's ward, and I remember my dear mother saying that you were fortunate indeed to have such a distinguished guardian."

"Fortunate indeed!" Mrs. Dempling had bristled at the words. "To have lost her parents in such a way! And so suddenly! Why, poor child, you must have been dreadfully unhappy."

"Yes, I was for a while," Mattie replied, smiling gratefully to her. "But His Grace was very good to me, and in time, I grew used to being an orphan."

Lady Repton had fallen silent then, but Mattie had read nothing upon her face except a certain envy.

As misplaced as this was, Mattie had immediately felt an easing in her chest. It was as if the burden of years had just been lifted, leaving her free to breathe deeply at last, for no censorious thoughts had accompanied Lady Repton's envy.

Everywhere Mattie had been since her arrival in Bath, she had been welcomed as if no scandal had ever attached itself to her name. People had been curious, perhaps, but that was natural with any newcomer. And how much more would they be with a duchess who had never appeared among them. Mattie had moved in society for a week and received nothing but attentiveness and kindness. Her fears of a lifetime had been groundless.

And here was Lady Repton, surely a stickler of the worst sort, rising and asking Mattie whether she would care to repair with her to the card-room.

"No, thank you," Mattie said with a perfectly clear conscience, although the thought of spending an evening playing cards with her ladyship made her toes go cold. "I am certain that Pamela would prefer to watch the dancers, and I must stay near her."

Lady Repton smiled that tight little smile

again. "So refreshing to meet a mother besides myself who observes all the proprieties. You will be glad for your sacrifice when you see your daughter's name held up as a model to others in future years." She curtsied her farewell. "I shall give myself the pleasure of calling upon you, duchess, to give you the benefit of my own experience as a parent."

Mattie thanked her, hoping desperately to be out when Lady Repton called, and nearly sighed out loud when she departed. Lady Repton had no sooner left the row of chairs than Mrs. Dempling scooted over to take the vacant place.

"Now we may be more comfortable," she said, settling into her new seat. "I have never liked that woman, if you will forgive my saying so."

Astonished by such candor, Mattie could only stammer, "Of course. I'm afraid—that is, I must admit that I found her conversation to be a bit tedious, if that is what you mean."

"Tedious?" Mrs. Dempling chuckled. "My dear, you are far too charitable. I can see it in your lovely face. Mean-spirited, I would sooner call her. But I'll leave off at the risk of sounding too much like her.

"How are you settling into Bath?" she asked.

Mattie was about to reply when Pamela goaded her with one elbow and made her jump.

"There's Gerald," Pamela whispered, and her face turned a deep, healthy rose, which would have soothed the worst of Mattie's maternal concerns if she were not anticipating William's arrival as well.

William had already entered the room, she saw, as she followed Pamela's glance. Interrupted in their chat, Mrs. Dempling followed it, too, and lit upon Gerald.

"Is that Lord Westbury's brother?" she asked. "I heard those two gentlemen were in town, but I could not imagine why. Is one of them ailing, do you suppose?"

Mattie feigned not to know, but she could feel the butterflies dancing in her stomach. "I have just made the gentlemen's acquaintance," she lied, forced to by William's idiotic charade. After Sir Reginald's resounding introduction in the Pump-room, she could not very well admit to an earlier familiarity without making everyone wonder about the cause for his deception.

Pamela must have heard Mattie's speech, for she threw her mother a bewildered glance. Fortunately, Gerald had seen the two of them and was making his way towards them.

"Hullo, Lady Pam, Your Grace." His casual attitude, even accompanied by a bow as it was, raised Mrs. Dempling's eyebrows.

"Good evening, Gerald." Mattie knew it was useless to pretend that Gerald was a stranger to either of them, especially without her daughter's complicity. And she could not ask for that, not without awakening Pamela's suspicions.

Drat William, she thought, for putting her in this most uncomfortable position. She had enough to worry her, what with all these new experiences, without having to manage that lie, too.

She explained to Mrs. Dempling that Westbury Manor, where she and Pamela had recently moved, abutted the country seat of Lord Westbury, and, consequently, that the two young people had made friends. Mrs. Dempling accepted this as Mattie had hoped she would, with the implication that Lord Westbury himself was still a relative stranger to them. Everyone seemed to know that William spent the greater part of his time in London, which made Mattie wonder what he had done to make his movements so well-known.

"Care to dance, Lady Pam?" Gerald offered his arm with a conspiratorial grin, which made Pamela blush and giggle.

Mattie intervened. "That is very kind of you, Gerald, but I am afraid that Pamela must not dance this evening, since she has not been brought out."

She felt a gentle nudge in the ribs. "Oh, go on, Your Grace." Mrs. Dempling smiled benevolently upon the young people and said, "What would be the harm in it? We are far from London, you know. Don't let that long-faced sourpuss spoil everyone's fun. She will try, you know."

"But I can't—" Mattie was in a quandary. She had already said that Pamela would not dance, and if she changed her mind, Lady Repton would surely be offended. At the same time, she had to agree with Mrs. Dempling that no harm could come of their dancing.

"That's quite all right, Your Grace," Gerald said, not in the least disturbed. "Lady Pam and I can wander about the room instead. We've got plans to make about our ride tomorrow. I want to show her a stud I promised she could see, and in the dance we would be interrupted again and again.

"All right by you, Lady Pam?" he asked.

Pamela gave her ready consent. Mattie knew that neither of them was addicted to dancing and would be just as happy sitting in a corner, discussing their outing. Pamela rose, bobbed a curtsy to Mrs. Dempling, and the two made off, arm in arm toward the refreshment tables.

"You will think it quite rude of me to say this," Mrs. Dempling whispered after them, "but I think there will be a match there someday."

Mattie turned to her, shock raising her voice an octave. "Oh, no," she protested. "Gerald is simply a friend of Pamela's. Quite a good friend, as it happens, but—"

Mrs. Dempling's knowing smile caused her to look inside herself. What Mattie saw there made her stop in midthought.

Pamela's strange behavior, her glumness, her want of energy—all these things had mocked Mattie's own behavior. What if Pamela was losing her heart to Gerald?

Anxiety had no sooner started its grip on her than a strangely warm feeling stole into Mattie's chest, bringing tears into her eyes. Gerald was a darling boy. He truly cared about Pamela, and they shared so many interests.

At once Mattie saw that her daughter could do no better than to choose a gentleman like him.

Pamela was young, of course, and she would have to complete a season in London first. Gerald himself had some growing up to do, his studies to finish. And yet he seemed to have matured considerably just since they had met him.

These reflections, and thoughts of her own stupidity, occupied Mattie's mind for a long moment, so that she was surprised to see William suddenly in front of her.

She looked up to find his dark gaze warming her, his subtle smile—no more than a slight lightening of his features—working its magic to give her heart a jolt.

He was accompanied by Mr. King.

After the gentlemen had bowed to both ladies, and Mr. King had presented William to Mattie's companion, the Master of the Ceremonies said with an arch look, "Your Grace, I have attempted to find this gentleman a partner, but Lord Westbury insists there is but one lady here tonight whom he cares to stand up with."

Mrs. Dempling gave a deep chuckle, and Mattie, whose cheeks had begun to heat, started to fan herself in rapid time. "Oh . . . indeed!" she said, trying to catch her breath.

"Yes, Your Grace. And as you may have surmised, that lady is yourself."

Mattie knew that she was blushing so furiously that the roots of her hair must have turned pink. Her heart was in turmoil. What could William mean by embarrassing her so?

"That is—that is very kind of his lordship to be so—so obliging to an old woman, but I am afraid—I—"

Mrs. Dempling chuckled louder. "My dear, how you do go on! Why don't you dance with the poor gentleman? I am certain I should if a gentleman half so handsome as this one made me a pretty compliment."

"Oh, no—" Mattie felt trapped. Here was William, staring down at her with his twisted smile that made her heart go aflutter, and these others looking on, who were certain to discover the truth about her feelings for him, if she was not extremely careful. "I do not think it would be proper in me to dance. At my age, one is only here to chaperon."

She had tried to make her voice sound firm, but apparently it did not, for she only drew another laugh.

"At your age? Well, if you do not wish to dance, my dear, then I should help to spare your blushes, but when I was your age, I could still perform a fair minuet." Mrs. Dempling patted her on the hand.

"But I am not well—"

"You are not? I am so sorry, dear, but there's such a pretty color to your cheeks. . . . Perhaps that is what fooled me."

"I perceive a generous ally in you, Mrs. Dempling." These were the first words William had uttered, and now he bowed to Mattie's companion. "I shall have to call upon you. Perhaps you can help me learn how to make my suit more persuasive."

She laughed indeed at that. "I doubt you stand in need of help, young man. I suspect you have a very persuasive way about you already. And your eyes have alighted upon the fairest damsel in the room, no matter that she is a widow."

"Precisely so."

At this point, Mr. King noticed that his services were needed elsewhere. "If I may be excused, Your Grace, Mrs. Dempling." He bowed and strolled away, leaving Mattie without a knight to turn to.

She had made the mistake of thinking Mrs.

Dempling to be her friend; now she discovered her in the other camp.

"Perhaps I should be going—" Mattie started to rise.

"Oh, I hope you will not," William said. "I was just about to ask you, since you seem so determined not to dance this evening, whether I might not fetch refreshments for you?"

The thought of sitting in a corner with William, and having him, perhaps, feed her each mouthful with his own fingers, made her weak at the knees. Her fears of society's displeasure had so recently been vanquished, she was not ready to court it again.

"I am afraid I cannot," Mattie said, still fanning herself rapidly. "Dr. Falconer has put me on a rigid regime. I am to eat nothing but hard biscuits and calf's-foot jelly for a week."

William's lips began to twitch. He moved closer to her, until their bodies just crossed, and said, soft and low, "Are you not afraid, duchess, that a week of such a drastic diet will make you woefully weak? So weak, in fact, that you would find it hard . . . perhaps impossible . . . to resist any outrageous suggestion that might be made to you?"

This possibility had never occurred to Mattie, but with William so close . . . so warm and close, it occurred strongly to her now. She found it quite probable, in fact. "If I find myself growing that weak," she vowed, swallowing with difficulty and taking a big step backward, "I will leave off with the diet directly."

"Ah. I see that you are resolved." William shook his head sadly. "Mrs. Dempling, do you see how resolute she is? She will neither dance with me, nor accept my offerings of refreshment. I hardly dare offer anything else, though I would heartily like to."

Mrs. Dempling tut-tutted. The traitress was enjoying this scene immensely. How dare William make fun of her like this!

"If you wish to do me a service, my lord," Mattie said almost tartly, "you might help me to find my daughter. She is with your brother."

"Gerald is having more luck than I? Is that what you imply?" William gave a sigh. "It is most unkind of you, duchess, to point this out to me. However, if what you truly wish is to find your daughter so you can depart, I will do all in my power to make it possible. Never let it be said that I denied you anything."

He turned to Mrs. Dempling to say good night. "While I am gone," he whispered over her hand, "I trust you will do whatever you can to further my good cause?"

She gave him her promise, and the two ladies watched him stroll in the direction of the card-rooms.

"What a charming suitor, my dear!" Mrs. Dempling said, looking after him. "So amusing! And so handsome! I wonder you do not swoon to have him look at you like that."

"Lord Westbury is only teasing." Mattie strove to recover her lost composure. She must not meet William like this again, not in the evening. The Pump-room had been bad enough, but this was much worse. She had more trouble resisting him when all the candles were lit and the light flickered over his masculine features and dark hair, and she could imagine they were alone, just the two of them. In spite of the people standing about them, she had had the illusion momentarily of being lost in a wilderness with him, and her instinct had been to reach out and hold on tight.

"Teasing?" Mrs. Dempling's doubting voice penetrated her thoughts. "His looks were anything but teasing. But perhaps you have been away from society so long, you do not recognize the signs. You may take my more experienced eye as witness. Lord Westbury looks like a man who knows what he wants."

Mattie's pulse began to race in her throat. She could not withhold an embarrassed smile. "Surely not. Such a thing would be most unusual."

"Why? Oh, you may be thinking of your age relative to his, but indeed, my dear, such things happen more often than you think. Why, dear Lord and Lady Holland were such a match."

Mattie's heart sank. "And as a result, I believe, neither one is received at Court."

Mrs. Dempling looked startled. "Oh, no, my dear. I am certain you are wrong. They are not received at Court, to be sure, but not because of her ladyship's age. No, it is rather due to her divorce."

And the resultant scandal, Mattie thought, though she said instead, "We have drifted far from the point, dear Mrs. Dempling. I am afraid you are exaggerating Lord Westbury's intent, and indeed, my own interest in him. It is most improper for me to discuss him in this way."

She could see that her new friend looked disappointed and not a little disapproving, which made her even sadder. But nothing would be served by discussing her reservations in public. Better to let Mrs. Dempling think that she did not welcome William's attentions.

Mattie found it much easier to be firm when William was not around.

He must have thought he had done enough damage for one evening, for he sent Pamela and Gerald to her and did not come again himself. Gerald escorted them to the door with many promises about the morrow and helped them into their sedan chairs. He insisted upon paying the fares in advance, saying that William had given him the money for them.

"He's such a dunderhead," Gerald said, "he thinks he somehow ran you off. But that's just foolish, isn't it, Your Grace?"

"Yes, of course it is," Mattie said, smiling as brightly as she could.

They bid Gerald good night. Mattie was grateful to have a chair to herself with the curtains drawn, so she could give in to her unhappiness without anyone's being the wiser.

## *Chapter Thirteen*

$\mathcal{T}$he next morning a box arrived just as Mattie sat down to breakfast.

"Who is it from?" Mattie asked, as Penworth, Lady Findlay's excellent butler, set it down beside her plate.

"There is a card attached, Your Grace." Searching for it, Penworth touched one gloved hand to his lips and, clearing his throat, added, "The parcel was brought round from the White Hart. The boy said to say, 'From an admirer.' "

"Ohhhh . . ." Recognizing William's bold hand in this, Mattie opened the box with trepidation. What could he be sending at this hour, and with such impertinence?

As soon as the seal was broken and the lid partially raised, a rich, sweet aroma escaped from the box, causing her to ask with delight, "Oh, what are they?"

"I believe," Penworth said, keeping his countenance admirably serious, "they are a local delicacy. Bath buns, Your Grace."

"Bath buns?" Mattie looked for the significance of William's gift, but it was difficult to think when faced with such a tempting smell. Melted sugar, a touch of spice. She touched one of the buns and its buttery icing stuck to her finger, which she then had to lick.

She closed her eyes and started to purr, the taste was so delicious. Then, remembering Penworth's rigid countenance, she hurriedly opened them again.

"Do you wish to read the card, Your Grace?" A muscle twitched in the corner of Penworth's mouth, but he bowed and extended it to her without breaking into a smile.

Just the thought of reading a missive from William caused Mattie's hand to shake. She took the envelope, wondering what audacious thing he would write.

She was not disappointed.

*Mattie, my love,*
  *You should put aside all thoughts of hard biscuits and feast on sweet buns with me.*
                                    *Eternally yours,*
                                    *William*

As blood pumped rapidly to her throat, and a warm, pooling feeling spread through her, Mattie murmured to herself, "Oh, you wicked, evil man!"

"I beg your pardon, Your Grace?"

Startled to find Penworth still standing beside her chair, she jerked erect and told him, "Nothing," before dismissing him quickly, knowing very well he had heard what she'd said. William's gift had been sent to tempt her from her resolve, but if he persisted in embarrassing her in front of the servants, she would have to refuse further gifts.

The aroma from the buns had wafted from the box and filled the room. Matttie put her head back, closed her eyes, and for a long moment, allowed herself to be seduced by the images it aroused: dining with William; breakfasting with William—she could almost see him in a brocaded dressing gown, perhaps with a touch of black stubble on his face from rising late. . . .

Pamela found her still dreaming when she bounced into the room, fresh and sunny-faced. Mattie sat back up with a start.

"Something smells good," Pamela said, coming down the length of the table to see what it was. "Oh, capital!" She reached for one. "Where'd you get those?"

Mattie watched her lick the sugar from her fingers and she sighed with longing. "Lord Westbury sent them around." It would not hurt to tell Pamela the truth this time, for she was used to William's kindnesses. But Mattie hid his note, and as soon as Pamela moved to the sideboard, she tucked it into the lace at her bosom.

The paper tickled her and made it hard to think.

I must not give in to those buns, she thought. Instantly she rang the bell and, when Penworth came, ordered a plate of hard biscuits and a cup of vinegar.

"A cup of vinegar, Your Grace?" Penworth acted as if he doubted his own hearing.

"Yes, vinegar. It is what my physician prescribed for me." This was not quite true. Dr. Falconer had said nothing about vinegar, but Mattie was sure he would concur with her antidote to William's sweetness.

"Are you feeling quite all right, Mattie?" Pamela had watched this interchange with concern.

"Yes, dear, you mustn't worry. I simply feel in the need of a—a sort of purging." When her vinegar arrived, Mattie tried to drink it, but could do no more than dip her biscuits lightly in it.

"Going to the Pump-room this morning?"

Mattie started to say yes, before she remembered that William would be there. She did not think she could face him without either weakening and giving in or becoming flustered and running away. "I think *not* today," she said.

"Are you certain everything is all right?" From Pamela, who thought the Pump-room very dull, this was an extraordinary show of concern.

"Yes, of course, dear." Mattie took pains to appear normal. "It is only that I wish to stay home to receive visitors today."

Ever since their names had appeared in *The Bath Chronicle* under the announcements of new arrivals, a steady stream of cards had been left by members of Bath society. Encouraged by the warm reception she had been given, Mattie thought she might enjoy having visitors. It was becoming apparent that being a duchess gave her an instant acceptance with those who liked to brag of their connections. More sincere friends would surely follow these. She had only to stay at home, and the problem with William would resolve itself.

Her excuse satisfied Pamela, who immediately after breakfast went upstairs to change into her riding habit. She and Gerald were to ride to Lansdown Hill to see its monument dedicated to the king's forces who had defeated the Parliamentarians there. Mattie had no objection to this outing. But with her new awareness of Pamela's feelings about Gerald, she had insisted that Lady Findlay's groom ride with them. The ease with which Pamela accepted this restriction told Mattie she had nothing to worry about.

Later, however, when Gerald arrived, it was hard to watch them mount their horses, knowing they would be gone for the better part of the day. Feeling lonely already, Mattie could not help but recall her pleasure in the outings she and William had shared with them.

When the groom led up the mount Gerald had brought for Pamela to ride, Mattie recognized it at once as William's own. "Is that not your brother's horse?" she asked.

"Yes, Your Grace." Gerald glanced at her before reddening and turning away. "You needn't think that Pam—Lady Pam, that is—cannot ride him. Believe me, Will would never have lent him to anyone else, but he says Lady Pam is the bruisingest rider he's ever seen, for a lady, that is. Anyway, we sort of—that is, *Will* had the idea that we ought to bring him just in case Lady Pam hadn't brought any horses of her own."

"That was very kind of your brother," Mattie said, hiding a smile at Gerald's ingenuousness.

"And you must thank him for sending those buns," Pamela added.

"What buns?"

Gerald appeared in the dark, so Mattie did her best to whisk the young people away. "Merely another kindness on his part. Do ride carefully, will you, please, and be back well in time to dress?"

Armed with their assurances, Mattie went back into the house fearing she would miss them both dreadfully.

A few visitors did call, which helped her to pass the morning, but the last one was still there when a bouquet of roses arrived.

Filled with delight, Mattie was on the point of burying her face in the blossoms when Penworth spoke. "A card is attached, Your Grace, but the man who brought them around said to inform you that Lord Westbury had sent them."

The possibility that the flowers were from William had already occurred to Mattie, and she had intended to wait until she was alone before opening the card. But Penworth's announcement had been made loudly enough to reach her visitor's ears.

"Westbury, eh?" The elderly general who had called gave a throaty chuckle that led to a wheeze. "Looks like you've made a conquest there, duchess." He coughed uncontrollably for a minute. "Can't say as I've ever heard of his pursuing a lady so publicly. Been a hard fish to catch, that one. But demned, if he didn't search the Pump-room for you this very morning! Left with his nose out of joint, or so I heard."

"Oh . . . I will not believe that." Mattie did her best to deny any knowledge of these sentiments, and it was true that she could not quite believe it. Where it was almost certain that William would have been disappointed not to see her, especially after sending her those buns—a thought that made her ache with guilt—he would never have shown his hurt unless he had wanted to achieve something by displaying it.

William seemed stubbornly determined that everyone should know he was pursuing her.

Mattie changed the subject as best she could and eventually showed her visitor out in the belief that she had distracted him and successfully squelched his gossip. After that, she had nothing to do but stare at a book until Pamela came home.

This she did in midafternoon, full of excitement over the vistas they had seen and eager to return on the tenth of August when a large horse fair would take place upon the down. Mattie gave her consent, hiding her sadness that she could not go out herself.

The guidebook she had purchased at a street stall promised her that Bath was "one of the most distinguished spots in the kingdom, where the Wealthy find every comfort and convenience and the Youthful can indulge in every rational pleasure." But Mattie knew she must not go anywhere, either to the Sydney Gardens or to the theater, which she had been longing to do, for fear that William might frequent such places. All shopping must cease or else she might run into him in Milsom or Bond Streets. Not even Mr. Gibbons's library in Argyle Street would be safe, for she might be seen through the glass.

She had to do everything in her power to overcome his latest tactics, for she could not bear for him to embarrass himself in public. Still, she was firm in her resolve that her difficulties would not interfere with Pamela's life.

But the next day, when again she did not go to

the Pump-room, another bouquet came from William, this time a much larger one of delicate, blue forget-me-nots. "From Lord Westbury again, Your Grace," Penworth announced.

Unfortunately, the visitor who witnessed this was Mrs. Dempling. She exclaimed over the flowers, wondering how Lord Westbury had managed to secure so many at this time of year. "For it is rather late in the summer, and I should think they would all have been burned up by now, as warm as it has been.

"But to be sure—" she threw Mattie an arch look "—he has taken great trouble to send these."

"I cannot—imagine why." Mattie tried to cover her confusion. It was said the forget-me-not should only be sent to one's truest love.

"Fie, my dear! You must think me a simpleton. And no need to pretend to be one yourself. Anyone can see that his lordship is heels over head in love with you."

"I know no such thing. Lord Westbury is merely—showing kindness to a neighbor."

"But such extreme kindness? Sending flowers two days in a row?"

Mattie started at this.

Mrs. Dempling gave her a nod. "Bath is a very small place, my dear. By the time the cardroom had closed at the Upper Rooms last night, everyone knew that his lordship had sent roses to you. And *everyone* knows what roses mean."

Agitated, Mattie could only look away. "Oh, Mrs. Dempling—you must not! You know what people would say if they thought such a foolish thing."

"Pooh! Let them say what they will. What does it matter?"

Her attitude astonished Mattie, who, not comprehending such indifference, could only stammer, "It matters a great deal."

Mrs. Dempling's face fell. When she spoke next, it was in a more reserved tone. "If that is what matters to you, Your Grace, then I apologize for my rudeness."

Mattie hastened to assure her that no offense had been taken, but she could see that Mrs. Dempling was disappointed in her. Unwilling for her behavior to go unexplained, she said, "It is not for me, but for my daughter's sake, that I must be so careful."

Mrs. Dempling merely gazed at her sadly. "And it is not for me to give you advice, my dear, so I will remain silent on that score."

Mattie thought her visitor had forgiven her, but Mrs. Dempling took herself away soon thereafter. Mattie turned her eyes to William's flowers, inhaled deeply to catch their scent, and thought about the time in her garden when he had kissed her.

Her garden would be a disaster now. She had left no instructions to her gardener, knowing he would not take the pains she had with it. Of a sudden, Mattie missed her flowers intolerably. She wanted to go back to the serenity she had found there, go back to the innocence she had known before William had come.

But then, her heart argued, you would have to give up the beautiful memory of his arms about you and those few moments of bliss before you discovered what he really wished.

She could not give those up. No matter how lonely and miserable she would feel from now on without him, she would not give up those moments.

William sent flowers every day that week. Bluebells for constancy, more roses for love, and lastly, crimson carnations for his ailing heart.

Seeing the progress Mattie had made, her new friends and admirers, he had thought that she would respond to his flower messages, if not to his other overtures. But, perhaps, insulated from society as she had been, she had not understood them. William was frustrated with waiting. He had made a cake of himself all over town, wearing his heart on his sleeve so she could not mistake the seriousness of his intentions. He, a noted Corinthian and, as some thought, peerless catch, had thrown his heart at her feet for all the world to see. It seemed she could not, or would not, realize that he did not mean to live without her.

He had to acknowledge that his Mattie was stubborn. He had driven her back into a sort of seclusion, which was the worst thing for her. He needed to rectify their course.

William decided it was time to stop acting the gentleman. He had not wished to bully her; he had given his promise that he would not. Mattie had enough neighbors and servants doing that already. William had preferred to give her his love. To teach her, in fact, what real love was about.

He thought by now she should have had a taste of society and should have learned that all her fears were pointless. But if she had not learned this on her own, then he would have to help her.

And if she would not respond to his more gentle urgings, she would have to listen to his more forceful ones.

He took up his hat, called for a chair, and went to see her in Upper Camden Place.

"I am afraid Her Grace has just gone out," her stately butler said, hiding the curiosity he surely must feel. William had given strict orders that his gifts were always to be announced, so he knew that Penworth was apprised of his efforts.

"Do you know where I might find her?" he asked, meaning to chase her down if he had to.

A visible struggle went on in the butler's mind before he answered, "I am not at liberty to say. However—" his voice softened imperceptibly "—if I might venture—the Lady Pamela is still at home if you would wish to pose that question to her."

"Thank you, Penworth." William stepped inside, aware that he had discovered another ally.

"I shall ask her to see you directly, if you would care to follow me. You may make yourself comfortable in the saloon."

William followed him as far as the next floor, but decided to stand by the stairs instead. He had not long to wait. Pamela came bouncing down within a few minutes.

"Hullo, your lordship."

Her unaffected greeting cheered William. "Hullo to you, Lady Pam." He watched her blush at Gerald's appellation for her. "I've been given to know that your mother is out. Do you know where she's gone?"

A cloud crossed Pamela's face. "Yes. You won't believe this, but she's gone to take the waters."

"To the Pump-room, do you mean?" After his waiting so patiently for a week when Mattie had not come, this was quite a turn.

"No. I mean she's taking a round of baths. She said her doctor prescribed them. Listen, Lord Westbury . . ." Pamela struggled to hide her concern. "You don't think Mama is really ill, do you?"

Laughter welled inside William, to think of Mattie's carrying her charade so far as to take a bathing cure. "No, I don't," he said. He could not hide his amusement entirely, but it seemed to comfort Pamela. "I simply think that your mother is determined to carry her own brand of quite charming lunacy a bit too far.

"You wouldn't happen to know which bath she is visiting?" he inquired, before Pamela could ask what he meant.

"Yes, I do. It's the King's Bath." Pamela seemed to remember something. "Mattie told me not to tell anyone where she had gone, but she couldn't have meant you, do you think?"

"Oh, surely not." William was at pains to hold his laughter inside. "Going for a ride with Gerald today?"

"Yes." Pamela colored, and it seemed to William that she had become almost beautiful. "We are riding to Claverton-down. To see some racehorses," she added hastily.

"What a splendid idea. Well, I wish I could accompany you, but I have business to attend in the center of town. You will say hello to my brother for me, will you not? I have not seen him this age, and cannot imagine where he has been keeping himself."

Since he knew very well that Gerald was practically living in Upper Camden Place, he was gratified by the blush with which Lady Pamela bid him good day.

Mattie was soaking up to her neck in the warm bath, her high-waisted bathing gown drifting languidly in the wake of every passerby.

She had found the bath to be another social meeting place. Though a few bathers were elderly and attended by nurses, an equal number seemed to have nothing much the matter with them. Ladies wore fetching bonnets with feathers flying above their drab, shiftlike gowns. Old dandies in cocked and high-crowned hats stood about in exaggerated postures. Some of the gentlemen were not above putting quizzing glasses to their eyes to ogle the younger women.

Seeing this, and wishing nothing more than to disappear, Mattie had found what she thought would be a subtle hiding place. But the cozy recess she had chosen behind a Doric colonnade had proved to be nothing less than a trap.

At the moment, she was doing her best to ignore the marked stares of three strange men who had followed her and stopped to chat, blocking her exit. They had watched her movements from the moment the attendant had opened the door to the bath from the ladies' quarters. Startled at first to see men sharing the bath with the ladies, Mattie had had no choice but to move among them. So far, none had approached her, but she was uncomfortably aware of being alone in a crowd, who seemed to have nothing better to do than flirt in the most outrageous way.

The water, too, was anything but refreshing. Warm and gray with a fine type of sand, it had a ponderous feel to it that made Mattie shiver with distaste. She was wondering how long she should stand before trying to make her way past the men when a familiar figure waded through them and glided straight towards her.

A bubble of relief filled her chest, and a smile broke across her face before she remembered that William was the man she had come here to avoid. Even as her heart beat in a flutter of irritation with herself, she could not help noticing how handsome he looked in his bathing garb.

On the other men, she had found the brown linens less than appealing, but with William's long, broad chest, the dampened shirt clung about his waist in a way that was most attractive. Mattie did her best to recall that she should be annoyed with him for coming, but it was hard to do when he stood staring down at her.

"Hello, Mattie," he said in an undervoice, a voice so low and intimate, it made her spine tingle. "What in heaven's name are you doing here?"

"I—am taking a cure. I told you that I was suffering from something. But what about you, Lord Westbury? I am astonished to see a gentleman as young and fit as yourself inside the baths."

Ignoring her question, William put his back to the wall, laid his hands on the stone seat behind him, and hoisted himself out of the water. His motion sent rivulets pouring from his torso and down his bent legs. Mattie gawked at the muscles in his arms, and then did everything in her power to prevent her eyes from falling to his Inexpressibles where the soaked material now clung in a most revealing way.

"Won't you sit here?" William said, patting the seat beside him. "I would be very pleased to help you up."

"William—Lord Westbury, how can you even suggest such a thing?" Mattie felt a flush rising to her temples. She put her hand to her lips to hide an outraged smile. If William's bathing dress fell in such a way, what would her own do?

"What?" William gazed innocently around the bath. "Oh, yes, I see the difficulty. You would not want all these other people to witness your *déshabillé*. And now that I think about it, neither would I, though I shall miss the pleasure myself."

"William, you mustn't talk in that fashion!"

"No? Then how should I talk to you, Mattie, so you will hear?"

Mattie felt an ache rising up inside her. She had not missed the gentle note of pain in his voice. "You know how I feel. And you know how futile this all is."

"Not at all." A flippant note had replaced the pain. "I think I will wear you down eventually.

"How did you like the flowers I sent you?" he asked before she could refute his statement.

"Oh . . ." Mattie could not keep her voice from softening. "They were so beautiful. All of them. I had them carried up to my room, so I—"

"Aha!" William's brow rose wickedly. "To your bedroom, do you mean?"

"Yes, but not because of what you think!" Mattie felt heated by her mistake. Now that William was here, the water's temperature had gone up by several degrees, and whereas before it had felt mildly oily and cloying, now it seemed like a pool of warm milk, silky and smooth and seductive. "I took the flowers up to my room because I thought their aroma might freshen the air. You know I have not been well, and it has long been thought that flowers soothe the invalid."

"Oh, I see. You must pardon me, duchess, but I have not yet heard what your symptoms might be."

William had the nerve then to put two fingers about his eye as if he had an ogling glass and to stare down at her figure in the water. "No, I see nothing glaringly missing, nor too much out of place, but it could be my eyesight in this dusky room."

"William, what *are* you doing here?"

"I have come to see whether you would attend the theater with me this evening."

Ohhhh . . . the wretch, Mattie thought. When he must know how much I would love to do just that. As much as it hurt to refuse him, Mattie stiffened her spine and said, "I cannot. I am afraid if I did, it would look somewhat particular."

"Which is exactly what it would be. I would not invite anyone else but you, now that I love you."

"William, please, you must respect my age and illness."

He clapped his palm to his forehead. "Alas, I forget again. Just what are you suffering from, Mattie?"

"From—from palpitations!" Mattie asserted indignantly, grasping at the first thing that came to mind.

"Ahhhhh . . ." The satisfied way William said this told her she had made a grave mistake. "Then I know the cure for that. Have I not told you that I suffer from palpitations, too, whenever you are near? But we can do something about that, Mattie."

"William . . . no." Mattie felt her breath coming in delightful little gasps. Her knees had grown weak. "We cannot—and you mustn't—" Then a light went off inside her head, and she thought, If William feels as weak about me as I do about him, then perhaps he will agree to an affaire after all.

"At least," she said, pitching her voice so low that no one else would ever hear and turning away to hide her own blushes, "there is something we might do, but I have already proposed it to you. . . ."

She trailed off on a note of inquiry. A second passed. Then another. And another, before William slid back into the water. Mattie felt him take her arm in a rigid grasp.

"Your Grace, you must let me escort you to the ladies' quarters before I take myself out of here. I am finding the air a little thick."

Mattie quaked at the suppressed anger in his tone. Cowed and ashamed, she allowed him to lead her to the other side of the room where an attendant waited to open the doors for her.

"Good day, Your Grace." William bowed his head to her before wading through the chest-high water to the gentlemen's quarters. Mattie would have watched him go but for the woman waiting to hand her up the steps. All she could do was drag herself up and away through the swinging doors with a heavy heart.

*Chapter Fourteen*

All the rest of that day, and throughout the night and the next morning, Mattie felt lost in a sea of misery. She had angered William. William, who had never shown her anything but gentleness and kindness, who had humbled himself to pursue her futilely in public, who had had the courage to bear public scorn. And whose only sin had been to fall in love with someone worse than a coward.

But had she been cowardly for herself? Her mind argued no, not as long as she was a mother and had Pamela to think of. Pamela must not be made to feel she was an outcast of society, not when living as a member of the ton had so many delights to offer her: the theater, the opera, the parties. Why, only this afternoon, Pamela had gone with friends on a visit to Sydney Gardens, which had been followed by a shopping expedition.

Outings such as these would be impossible if Pamela's mother disgraced herself. The feeling of knowing that each person she passed was whispering about her was so painfully fresh to Mattie that it might have happened yesterday instead of twenty years ago. She could not bear the thought of Pamela's suffering the same estrangement.

But to realize how much she had hurt William, whom she loved—she, who had always tried to spare the feelings of others—was almost more than Mattie could stand. His steely expression, the cold light in his eyes as he had bid her good day, the hurt in his tone, drowned all other thoughts and feelings from her mind, so that she was startled to hear Pamela address her by name.

"Mattie?" Pamela had entered the parlor some time before, but Mattie had been so swamped with unhappiness, she had not noticed how unusually quiet her daughter was.

"Yes, dearest, what is it?" Her concern aroused, Mattie sprang to alertness.

"Oh, it's nothing, I suppose. . . ."

Now Mattie truly was alarmed. Pamela had never been one for reticence. "Darling, you must tell me. I can see that something has overset you."

"Well . . ."

Mattie could feel Pamela's struggle, and the thought of her daughter's mind in turmoil brought out her most protective instincts. "Go on," she said, trying to sound calm.

"Well, I was in a shop in Milsom Street, and I overheard two ladies talking."

"Yes . . ."

"They were talking about you."

A pang shot through Mattie's heart. "What were they saying?"

Pamela squirmed uncomfortably. "It was about Lord Westbury, too."

Oh, dear Lord. Mattie suddenly realized she had been so intent upon hiding herself that this possibility had never entered her mind. She should have known that eventually some of the gossip would make it to Pamela's ears.

"What were they saying, dear?" Mattie tried to act as if nothing anyone could say would ever bother her. "And who were they?" Pamela must not grow up being afraid of her own shadow.

"It was Lady Repton and one of her friends. They said . . ." Pamela paused, and then went on with her cheeks aflame, "They said that Lord Westbury was in love with you and that you were leading him on a sad dance."

Mattie gave a high, false laugh. "What an absurd bit of gossip. Is that all they said?"

"No." Pamela did not offer to repeat the rest. "But they did not sound as if they approved of your behavior to him."

"Pamela, dear—" Mattie assumed the firmest tone she had ever used with her daughter "—you must not let other people's approval or disapproval disturb you."

"Oh, I didn't." The surprise in Pamela's voice rang astonishingly true. "It is just . . . Don't you like Lord Westbury?" The look accompanying her question turned it into an accusation, which took Mattie aback.

"Yes, of course. Of course I like him. Very much. He is one of the—kindest, the most honorable, the most considerate gentleman of my acquaintance." Her heart nearly melted to acknowledge it.

"Then why won't you marry him if he wants?"

"Marry?" Pamela's incomprehension startled

her. "Why, because he is younger than I am, dear."

Pamela's brows rose. "Is he? He doesn't seem like it to me, and I think he is fond of you."

"It is possible that he is," Mattie admitted, shaking inwardly, "but I am afraid that does not necessarily make us suitable partners."

Pamela's face crumpled in a confusion behind which Mattie could read disappointment in herself. She tried to make Pamela understand.

"Darling, if I were to marry Lord Westbury, then people would say I had robbed the cradle. Some people might be quite unpleasant about it indeed."

"Yes . . . ?" Pamela was looking at her as if to say, What would that matter?

Mattie started to speak. She hesitated when she found her own words to Pamela coming back at her, those brave words about not letting what people said determine her own happiness. Mattie found that she could not defend her conduct without going against every lesson she wanted Pamela to learn.

Looking at Pamela now, she felt an instant revelation. This daughter she had raised so far from society had created a happiness all her own. Pamela had not needed the balls and gowns, the admiring friends, or the approval of great ladies to forge her success. She had pursued the things she loved and found a soul mate in the process.

A bell sounded deep inside Mattie, a sound that mingled with a dawning indignation over Lady Repton's gossip. How dare that woman criticize her for discouraging William when she would be among the first to be outraged if Mattie accepted him?

And how dare Lady Westbury accuse her of ensnaring her son when nothing had been further from Mattie's mind?

This thought, that there were some people who would talk spitefully about her no matter what she did, no matter how worthy her intentions, hit Mattie soundly in the face. Mattie knew suddenly that she could never please Lady Repton or her ilk. And why should she bother, when she did not particularly care for the woman in the first place?

She had only been harming herself and hurting William, her dearest love, in an effort to please those filled with spite. A feeling of relief washed through her, a feeling of lightness and giddiness and hope. It was instantly followed by an anxiety so fierce, it gripped her stomach. What would she do in the event she had given William such a disgust of her that he would never propose again?

William had quickly recovered from his anger, an anger that had stemmed as much from frustration as from anything else. It had been almost more than he could bear to stand so close to Mattie in the baths and not make love to her. Then, to find that, in spite of all his efforts, they were right back where they had started had overset his normal control. He had wanted nothing more than to shake Mattie until her teeth rattled, to see whether a stronger tactic would show her how foolish she was being.

By the time he had reached the White Hart,

this desire had burned itself out in the grinding of his teeth. A pint of Mr. Woodhouse's best bitters soon cooled his temper, and William was able to think about what he should do next.

He had tried patience and cajolery. Pressure had failed, but he was not reduced to begging, yet. He knew that Mattie loved and wanted him, else she would never have made such an outrageous offer, one that made light of his feelings for her. He wondered if, perhaps, Mattie's problem was that she doubted how strong those feelings were.

To provide her reassurance, he would need to show her the depth of his passion. He would need to talk to her, and not just in snatches like the one they had shared today, but in long, leisurely talks, more like the ones they used to have in the country.

With one important difference.

William knew that as a last resort, he could always use pity to trap Mattie's tender heart, but there was still one last weapon he had not used, and that was one he infinitely preferred.

He had learned early in his manhood that to engage a lady's sentiments too deeply, when he had no serious intention of returning them, was not only cruel, it was a mistake. Since discovering this danger, he had been careful that his attentions were never particular enough to be misconstrued, his ardor never fervent enough to lure anyone's heart to self-destruction.

But this case was different. If he wanted to win Mattie, he would have to put off his cool exterior and show her what their lives could be in each other's arms.

And to show her that, William realized as he sought his sheets that night, he just might have to resort to a little trickery.

His pulse raced with the anticipated pleasure of executing his plan. By hook or by crook, he would get Mattie into his arms, and when he was finished with her, he'd be damned if she refused him again.

The next morning, her knees shaking with her own daring, Mattie was preparing to take a chair to the Pump-room to find William when Penworth announced a visitor. Her impulse to curse at the interruption was quickly stifled by the information that it was William who awaited her in the parlor.

Her breath caught in her throat. A wild hammering started deep in the center of her chest. Mattie put one hand to a chairback to still her dizziness.

"You may tell Lord Westbury," she said breathlessly, "that I shall be down in one moment."

"Yes, Your Grace." Penworth bowed in his impeccable fashion. "Should I ask Cook to prepare anything to serve?"

"No!" Mattie had a horrifying vision of how embarrassing it would be if Penworth walked into the room just after William proposed again. If William did—and Mattie was determined to do what she could to induce him—she planned to throw herself directly in his arms. And then ...

But she was getting ahead of herself. And Penworth was staring at her as if some explanation was warranted for such a negative order.

"We—that is, Lord Westbury's business may

not take very long. And if it does . . . then we shall simply ring for something later."

Penworth bowed. "As you say, Your Grace." His features were composed, and Mattie was relieved to see not a trace of curiosity upon them.

He descended the stairs, and Mattie made a quick check in the mirror to see how she looked.

She was dressed in a light muslin gown, covered in pale pink bouquets bound with blue ribbons, precisely the colors William had told her she should wear. Since her purpose had been to look as young as possible this morning, she had put her hair up simply. Now that she did not mean to go out, she removed her straw bonnet and tucked the loose strands back in place. Checking for gray hairs, Mattie was pleased to see none. She lifted her chin and tested the firm skin underneath, then sucked in her stomach.

Finding it difficult to breathe this way, especially as nervous as she was, Mattie let her stomach back out and hoped that William could love her with a bulge as much as without. Finally she girded herself and made her way downstairs.

William was standing by the window when she came into the room. He turned when he heard her, but stood away and regarded her soberly.

"Mattie . . ." As soon as the door was closed behind her, he started to speak. "I am glad you agreed to see me."

"But of course I would." Mattie tried to keep her voice from trembling, though her knees shook. How *did* one tell a man one was ready to accept him?

William's features softened slightly. He took

one step closer. "I have thought and thought about your offer . . ." he began.

Mattie started to interrupt him with a protest, but he finished too quickly ". . . and I have decided that perhaps you are right."

"You have?" Mattie's heart sank. "You mean . . . ?"

"Yes." William took several steps closer now. "I do want you for my mistress. I have to have you, Mattie."

"Ohhh . . ." Disappointment seized her like a vise, but she did not dare show it. If William took her that way, she had only herself to blame. The dreams she had indulged in all night—going to the theater and the opera in London with William, seeing him at all hours of the day, riding in his carriage and openly holding hands—all faded into mist. The pleasure that she was sure they would have in William's bed, or wherever their affaire would take place, though wondrous, would make a pale second to the far more lasting joy of being his wife.

Mattie swallowed and allowed William close enough to take her into his arms. The warmth of his embrace made tears rise to her eyes.

"What do you say, Mattie?" he asked, whispering softly in her ear. "Will you become mine?"

Mattie could not answer. His voice so low and gentle was making music in her veins, but such a sad music. Like the voices of sirens on the shore, it lured her to her doom.

To see William like this. Hiding. Always hiding behind closed doors . . .

He raised her chin slowly with one finger and kissed her. Mattie felt her lips melting from the heat of his, her pulse racing to meet the beat of his heart, so closely pressed to hers.

But what if someone were to discover them? She nearly jumped in his arms. What could she tell Pamela?

"Mattie . . ." The passion in William's voice reverberated through her, turning her knees to jelly.

When he held her this way, when he showed her the depth of his passion, she knew he might do with her what he willed and she would not care if the whole world were watching.

But—but what about breakfasting with William, and dining with William, and all those other things she wanted?

With a start, Mattie opened her eyes and shoved him away.

"What—" William's brows snapped together. "What is it, Mattie? I thought this was what you wanted."

"I did. At least, I thought I did, but—" A new courage filled her. William could have her, but only if he took her the right way. "I thought I did, so it is not your fault," she said justly, though she wanted to cry at her mistake. Why had she not accepted him before?

"But I've changed my mind," she continued. "I find that I cannot be your mistress. If you want me, you will have to take me to wife."

"I—" William's brows lifted in surprise. His lips gave a twitch. "I shall have to do what?"

"You will have to marry me, I'm afraid. I have discovered that I am not that sort of woman."

He was struggling not to laugh now. She could

see it in his face before he folded her back in his arms.

"Now, what sort of woman is that?" he asked teasingly. "The sort that would run from a gentleman's proposals? The kind that would torture me for days by hiding from me? Or maybe the kind that would insist that I conceal my feelings for her?"

Mattie blushed at the chronicle of her sins. "No, I admit that I was all those things, but I needed time to—"

"Time to what?" William grew more sober. "Time to believe how deeply I love you, and how I will never let anyone hurt you again?"

"No, not that." William's hands were drawing swirls on her back that made her quiver. "More that I needed to realize how very much I love *you*, which is far more than I could love any other person—except Pamela, of course—and that I should try to make you happy rather than all those others."

"But you would, Mattie. I am certain that, as my mistress, you would make me more than happy." William gave her a leer that almost made her shriek.

"No, I wouldn't. For I would not be happy except as your wife, so you needn't tease me any longer, William, or I shall ask you to remove your hands from where they are!"

"My, my, but we are becoming forceful! Have I been deceived in my bride? Quite the bully you've become lately, insisting upon this and that, marriage and whatnot. . . ."

In spite of his still-teasing note, Mattie faltered momentarily. "You do not mean that, do you, William? I know you had changed your mind, but I now know that such an arrangement would be a grave mistake. Why, think of what people would say if they ever found out! Think of what it would do to Pamela!

"And that's another thing! You may not have noticed, dearest, but Pamela and Gerald have become quite ... well, let us say that they have become chums. So close, in fact, that I've even wondered whether they might not—"

"No!" William's astonishment sounded a trifle false.

"Yes, indeed they have. And if such a thing were to come to pass, then how evil it would sound if anyone were to hear that his brother and her mother ..."

William's shoulders shook. He lowered his head to one side of hers, and Mattie felt an instant thrill down her spine.

"William, what are you doing!"

"I am nibbling on your ear because you are so adorable. Do you mind?"

"Um ... no."

"Good. Then I suggest we stop talking about Pamela and Gerald unless you mean to tell me that considerations of their respectability were the only reasons you decided to marry me."

"Oh, but they weren't!" Mattie held on to his lapels, while his nuzzlings brought irresistible giggles to her throat. "I am very much marrying you for what I want."

"Which is ... ?"

"I want to go to the theater in London."

"All the way to London? Well ... I shall have to see what I can do. ..."

"And I think I want to travel, but not too far at first, in case I do not like it."

"Oh, you will like it. I shall make certain that you do. Anything else?"

"William . . ." Mattie tried to sober him for a few minutes, but the task was hard . . . "You *do* still want to marry me, don't you? I did not use coercion?"

"If you mean, did you tempt me beyond reason and then withhold what I wanted, then I should think 'seduction' would be the more appropriate term. But no—" he held her away so that she could see the seriousness behind his smile "—you did not force me, my darling. I had no intention of taking you to bed without a wedding license, signed and sealed by the Archbishop of Canterbury himself."

The depth of his gaze told her that he meant what he had said. "Then earlier . . . you were lying?"

"Yes indeed. But before you take me to task, remember what a pretty dance you have led me, and tell me then I had no right to use trickery."

"When were you going to tell me the truth?"

"As soon as I heard you gasp my name aloud."

"William! What a shocking thing to say!"

He laughed with his head thrown back. Mattie had never seen him so happy, and to think that she was responsible for his happiness raised bubbles of joy inside her and brought fresh tears to her eyes.

"Do you think it shocking? Well, I assure you, duchess, that it will become so commonplace about our house that you will soon think nothing of it."

"Truly?" Mattie traced William's lips with her fingertips and wonder filled her voice. "Do you know, I think I shall enjoy being married to a younger man very much."